Young Lions

The Collins Book of Stories
for Six-Year-Olds

The Collins Book of Stories for Six-Year-Olds

Collected by Julia Eccleshare

Illustrated by Beryl Sanders

Young Lions
An Imprint of HarperCollins Publishers

Acknowledgements

The publishers are grateful to the following for
permission to reproduce copyright material:

Kenneth Kaunda Foundation for *Suspicion Spreads*
retold by Charles Vyas; Zimbabwe Publishing House
for *Den of the Reptile* by Daniel Motsi;
Laura Cecil Agency for *Tea at Mrs Manderby's*
by Adèle Geras

First published in Great Britain as
*Tobie and the Face Merchant and Other Stories
for Six-Year-Olds* by HarperCollins 1991
First published in Young Lions1991
3 5 7 9 10 8 6 4

Young Lions is an imprint of the Children's Division,
part of HarperCollins Publishers Ltd,
77–85 Fulham Palace Road,
Hammersmith, London W6 8JB

Collection copyright © Julia Eccleshare 1991
Illustrations copyright © Beryl Sanders 1991

Copyright in the individual stories remains
the property of each author

The authors assert the moral right to
be identified as the authors of this work

ISBN 0-00-673230-5

Set in Ehrhardt
Printed and bound in Great Britain by
HarperCollins Manufacturing, Glasgow

Contents

Tobie and the Face Merchant

by Adam Munthe

Tobie woke up on Monday morning and got dressed for school. He had breakfast, washed his face, brushed his teeth, and decided something was seriously wrong with his face.

"I don't like it," he told his mother. "I looked in the mirror and it's horrid."

"It's silly," he told his father. "People just laugh at it."

"It's not fair," he told his brother. "Yours is better."

When he got back from school Tobie decided that the situation was impossible. He frowned terribly.

"It's only because you feel miserable when you decide to look in the mirror," said his mother.

"People laugh because you're funny, not because your face is," said his father.

"Never mind," said his brother. "You can't help it. I'd get a new one if I were you." He should have known better, but he couldn't help being an elder brother.

"The shop's down the street," Tobie told his mother on Saturday morning. "I'm going after breakfast, and they sell them in all colours."

"How nice," she said, cleaning her palette with turps. "Why don't you get some balloons too? Cross on the zebra, please."

Tobie always looked left and right in case any flying saucers were passing. Today there were no cars either, so he crossed on the zebra crossing. "Funny," he said to himself, "that a seven-year-old boy hasn't even seen *one* flying saucer."

In the window it just said "New Faces for Old – (good cash incentives)". Tobie walked straight in and the doorbell jangled. The man at the counter reminded Tobie of an alligator. He couldn't actually see the tail but that was probably why the man wore long overalls.

"Faces?" said Tobie.

The man smiled and pointed at the racks of faces. They lay in boxes like fruit at the greengrocer's. "Just choose one you fancy, and afterwards we'll make the exchange."

Tobie thought the man's fingernails were far too long, and unnecessarily dirty.

"Is three weeks' pocket money enough for a new face?" he said.

"More than enough," said the alligator gentleman.

Tobie moved along the racks.

The one he picked had hair as well, but no ears. The hair wasn't spiky at all, the nose didn't turn up, the mouth wasn't crooked and laughing, the chin wasn't dimpled, and the eye-holes were not crinkly at the sides and almond-shaped. Perfect, in fact.

"I'll have to keep my own ears," said Tobie. "Will you wrap it up, please."

"No need," said the man, and he came round the counter. With one lightning movement he peeled off Tobie's face, right down to the chin. The new one was in place in a jiffy. "And what's more, we're having a sale, so it's only two weeks' pocket money, and your old face of course." He smiled nicely. "Unless you want new ears too."

"That's enough changes for one day," said Tobie with a slightly muffled voice. His new lips were difficult to talk through, and he didn't see the notice inside the door as he left.

Tobie's brother, coming down the road on his bicycle, didn't recognise him.

Tobie's father, playing Schubert on the piano (with quite a few false notes), didn't recognise him.

Tobie's mother at her easel said "Who are you?" and then covered her mouth with both hands so as not to scream.

"How did you have recognise me?" said Tobie sadly through his new lips. The lips worked better with practice.

"What have you done?" said his mother.

"Was it my green eyes?"

"It was your earlobes with the dents in them," said his mother distractedly. "What are we going to do?"

"Nothing," said Tobie. "Whose pocket money was it after all?"

"We're going straight back to the shop," said Tobie's father. "How could you?"

Tobie's brother looked sheepish.

The alligator gentleman listened carefully, and then went behind the door and brought back the little notice. It said in very small letters:

EXCHANGES BUT NO REFUNDS (COUNCIL TRADING LAW 239A)

"And it's closing time, I'm afraid," he said.

They walked home in silence.

"Do you think it used to belong to somebody else?" said Tobie, later, "or was it made for the occasion?"

"Probably," said his father.

The next day Tobie went over the square to see Alex. Alex was a girl. In fact she was one of the girls he might marry when he grew up. He rang the bell.

"How stupid!" said Alex when she opened the door. "You just fell for it, didn't you!"

She looked exasperated.

"Hook, line and sinker," she said.

Tobie had a sinking feeling. "You couldn't have recognised me," he shouted.

"Stupid!" said Alex, "and don't shout!"

"Stop saying stupid," shouted Tobie.

"Your stupid old eyes are behind your stupid new face, and I . . ." Alex paused for effect, "*know* them. And behind the stupid old eyes is stupid old you, and I know *you*!"

"So what's the point in having a new face?" said Tobie.

"So that new people don't recognise

you, I suppose," said Alex, with tears in her eyes, and slammed the door in his face.

"I like my new face!" Tobie said accusingly through the letterbox. But there was no answer.

"Did you ever think of changing your face?" Tobie asked.

"Yes," said his brother, pulling on his new football boots, "but I didn't."

"I'll play with you if you tell me about the Face-man," said Tobie.

"All right," said his brother. "He's a cheat. Selling people new faces and taking away their old faces is pretending that they can be new people. And I'll be goalie first."

"Exactly," said Tobie. "That's why I changed, and also because my old face was ugly."

"Yes," said his brother. "I agree completely, but is it any better now?"

Tobie threw the football at him.

Alex and her parents and a French lady with a double-barrelled name came for lunch.

"She's apt to be critical," said Tobie's mother beforehand, "so don't lick your plate in front of her."

"What's 'apt'," asked Tobie, "and 'critical'?" No answer as usual, he thought.

Alex's parents looked surprised all through lunch.

Tobie's father forgot to make conversation.

Tobie's mother had red eyes, and kept looking at the dents in his earlobes.

But the French lady told everybody what a nice, sensible, serious child he looked. "Good strong nose like Napoleon," she said. "Well-developed features for a small person, like a court dwarf I once knew."

"What's a court dwarf?" asked Tobie.

"And where did he get that splendid chin and firm jawline from?" she said.

"I'm not a dwarf," said Tobie very loudly, "and I bought it all from the Face-man next to the sweet-shop. It's not mine, really."

His mother clapped a hand over his

mouth. "He's joking," she said.

"No he's not!" said Alex scornfully.

So Tobie licked his plate in front of everybody.

"It's not so bad," said his brother that night when they went to bed. "You could buy a few more and change them during music lessons. Mrs Murphy might have a fit and leave."

"No more music lessons!" said Tobie. "That'd be good."

"If you changed faces enough you'd become almost invisible."

"That's good too, I suppose," said Tobie.

"No one would ever recognise you."

There was silence in the dark. His brother slept, and Tobie watched the reflections from the street lamp and the car lights swaying over the walls in his room. He felt that he might disappear into a new face, and that he wouldn't recognise himself any more. "But Alex would know," he said to himself, "wouldn't she?"

On Sunday morning his father took him to the National Portrait Gallery all by himself, without his elder brother. They stopped in front of a picture of a man in a red cap with a little boy.

"Ghirlandaio," said his father absent-mindedly.

"Poor man," said Tobie, "look at the bobbles on his nose. And the size of it."

"Exactly!" said his father.

They sat down in front of the picture to eat their crisps.

"But he's got kind eyes," said Tobie, "and you'd feel safe with him."

"Yes," said his father.

"And I think the little boy must love him."

On Monday, Tobie's father didn't go to the office. He went to the town hall instead, with Tobie. Afterwards a small man with a bald head took them to the Face-man's shop. Tobie's father pointed out the small notice just inside the door.

"Not regulation lettering," said the bald man from the town hall.

The alligator gentleman smiled.

"And not prominently situated," added the bald man.

The alligator gentleman stopped smiling.

"Therefore business transactions performed in the circumstances may be considered void." (Which meant that the Face-man had to give Tobie back his face.)

"Thank you," said Tobie's father, and sighed.

"Rules are rules," said the bald man.

"Argh!" shouted the alligator gentleman, grinding his teeth ferociously.

"What do 'prominently', 'transactions', and 'void' mean?" asked Tobie. He put his old face back on all by himself.

"For the first few days," said his mother, when they got home, "only use the mirror when you're feeling happy!"

"I agree," said Tobie, and he rang Alex on the telephone. "It's me," he said.

"Which one?" snorted Alex.

He thought for a while. "The original!"

"In that case," said Alex, "come for breakfast."

"Good word, that!" he told himself afterwards.

That night Tobie practised squinting, frowning, gargling, and looking miserable, in the bathroom mirror. Then he tried looking straight into his own eyes.

"Just watch it!" said Tobie.

And he went to bed.

The Wishing Fish Clock

by Joyce Dunbar

In the town of Cheltenham there is a shopping arcade.

In the shopping arcade there is a clock. It is called the "Wishing Fish Clock".

At the top of the clock there is a white duck that lays golden eggs.

At the bottom of the clock, like a pendulum, there is a great wooden fish with a wide open mouth. This fish is as big as a boat. Every hour, on the hour, he plays a tune – "I'm For Ever Blowing Bubbles".

His eyes switch on and off, his fins flip to and fro, and bubbles pour out of his mouth.

There is a mouse that goes in and out of doors at the sides of the clock, and a snake that tries to eat the mouse. The snake would like to steal the golden eggs. The snake never gets the mouse, and he never gets near the golden eggs.

This makes him feel very spiteful!

He is a spiteful yellow and green, with a wicked forked tongue and red eyes. But the mouse doesn't know he is there and the duck isn't worried about her eggs.

A brass sun on the big hand of the clock smiles all the time at passers-by. The minute hand is a crescent moon. The clock hangs high up on the wall, way above people's heads. But they always stop to stare at the clock, and when they see the mouse that goes in and out, and the duck that lays golden eggs, their faces light up and they smile. They forget about their shopping for a while and remember something long lost.

As for the children – every hour, near

the hour, they gather under the clock. They count the seconds ticking by. There! It's four o'clock! The clock face goes into a spin, with painted animals chasing each other. The fish plays his tune and blows his bubbles. Then, laughing and clapping and leaping in the air, the children catch every one. For each bubble they can burst they get a wish.

The duck and the fish and the mouse love the shopping arcade. They love it by day when the sun gilds the great glass-domed roof and they love it when the moon makes it silver. The snake likes it best in the dark. Then he tries harder than ever to eat the mouse and steal the golden eggs.

The duck and the fish and the mouse love watching the people down below.

"See how their faces light up!" says the duck.

"Look how they smile!" says the fish.

"Aren't people—" says the mouse, popping out, but he can never finish his sentence because he has to go in again, "*won-*

derful!" he says, inside the clock.

But the snake looks sly and stays silent. He is waiting for his chance.

One evening, when there was neither sun nor moon and all the shoppers had gone home, a different sort of person came along.

He didn't look up at the clock but kept his gaze fixed on the ground. He didn't look into the shop windows, but kept his hands deep in his pockets. At eight o'clock, when the painted animals started chasing each other and the fish played his tune and blew his bubbles, he did not smile at all.

This person was a tramp. He had no home to go to, no bed to sleep in and no food to eat.

"Why are you so unhappy?" said the fish, with a mouth full of bubbles.

"I think it's because of the world," said the tramp.

"What's wrong with the world?" asked the fish.

"That," said the tramp, "would be telling."

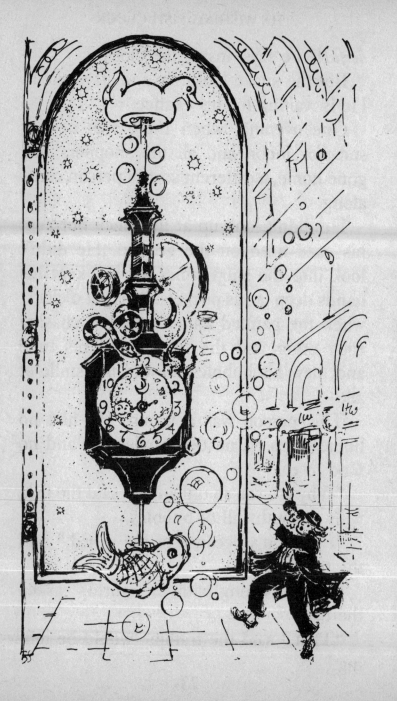

"I thought *this* was the world," said the duck.

"Well, it isn't," said the tramp. "This is a shopping arcade. The world is all outside."

"Aren't people—" said the mouse, popping out, "*wonderful*!" he said, popping in.

The tramp just shrugged his shoulders.

"Tell us about the world," said the fish.

"It is not what it seems," said the tramp.

"I *know*!" hissed the snake.

"What do you *mean*?" asked the fish.

"Aren't people—" said the mouse, popping out of the door near the snake, "*wonderful*!" he said, popping in.

The snake hissed, snatched and missed.

"People are not what they seem," said the tramp.

"I *know*!" hissed the snake.

"What do you *mean*?" asked the fish.

The tramp looked thoughtful for a moment. "Out there in the world," he began, "there are other creatures like you – marvellous creatures called whales. They don't hang on a wall. They swim in the wide vast oceans. They sing songs that echo in the deeps. Great water spouts gush from their heads. These creatures are in danger—"

"Danger?" said the fish.

"They are in danger from people!" said the tramp.

"Are there other creatures like me?" said the duck.

"Ah," said the tramp, shaking his head, "there are other creatures like you – magnificent creatures called eagles. They don't sit on top of a clock. They soar in the highest skies. They are not tame like you, but fierce and wild and free. These creatures are in danger—"

"Danger?" said the duck.

"People steal their eggs," said the tramp.

"How?" hissed the snake.

"Are there other creatures—" said the mouse, popping out, "like me?" he said, popping in.

"Yes, there are!" shouted the tramp, so that he could be heard inside the clock. "Millions of creatures like you, and some that are very much bigger. Enormous gigantic elephants! They do not live in a clock. They live in the thickest jungle. The elephants are also in danger."

"Are we in danger too?" asked the mouse, staying out longer than usual.

The snake hissed, snatched and missed.

"Perhaps not," said the tramp.

"You must bring all the whales to see me!" said the fish.

"And all the eagles to see me!" said the duck.

"And the elephants—" said the mouse, popping out, "to see me," he said, popping in.

"We will warn them!" said the fish.

"You don't understand!" said the tramp. "One single whale would fill the whole of the shopping arcade. An elephant would go thundering through it. He might smash all the shop windows! And the eagle—"

"What would the eagle do?" asked the duck.

"The eagle might eat that snake," said the tramp.

"You must bring them just the same!"

said the fish, the mouse and the duck.

"You don't understand!" said the tramp. "The whales need the sea! The eagles need the sky! The elephants need the jungle!"

"Then you must bring the sea to see me," said the fish, "and I will teach it to blow bubbles."

"And you must bring the sky to see me," said the duck, "and I will teach it to lay eggs!"

"And you must bring the jungle to see me," said the mouse, managing to stay out all the while, "and I will teach it to go in and out!"

"The sea blowing bubbles! The sky laying eggs! The jungle going in and out!" said the tramp, hopping from one leg to the other with the difficulty of it all. "That's not the answer to anything! That wouldn't solve a single thing! It's *people* that cause all the trouble! It's *people* you need to teach! And *people* will never learn!"

"I *know*!" hissed the snake.

"What about the children?" asked the fish.

"Children are all very well," said the tramp, "but they mostly grow up to be *people*!"

The tramp was getting really worked up. He paced up and down the arcade, his voice getting louder and louder.

"*People* are a very great *puzzle*! *Somebody* should do *something* about it!"

"Aren't you a people?" said the fish.

"I am," said the tramp.

"And is what you say quite true?" said the duck.

"It is," said the tramp.

"And is there nothing—" said the mouse, popping out, "we can do?" he said, popping in.

"Nothing," said the tramp.

"Can't you wish?" said the Fish.

"Wishes won't help," said the tramp.

"Then I will stop blowing bubbles," said the fish.

"And I will stop laying eggs," said the duck.

"And I will stop going in and out," said the mouse.

And the mouse stayed out, right under the eyes of the snake, right under his spiteful forked tongue. The mouse stayed there, very very still. Close by him was a golden egg.

The snake arched his long thin neck. He hissed his terrible hiss. He stretched out his deadly tongue. He was poised, ready to strike!

But suddenly, the whole clock stopped.

The snake was forced to stop too. Oh, what spite in his eyes! And oh, what fear in the mouse!

The tramp was completely dumbfounded. He didn't know what to do.

"No, no, it's not true. . ." he began saying to the clock.

"Come on now, move along there. You know you're not allowed to sleep in here," said another voice.

It was a policeman, talking to the tramp.

"But the clock!" said the tramp.

"What about the clock?" said the policeman.

"It's stopped!" said the tramp.

"Well, there's not much you can do about it," said the policeman.

"You don't understand," said the tramp. "It's my fault the clock has stopped! I have made it despair!"

"Move along there," said the policeman, and he began pushing the tramp out of the arcade, out into the cold dark night, where there was neither sun nor moon.

"It's not true!" yelled out the tramp. "It's not true what I said about the world! It's a story! I made it all up! The world is a shopping arcade! What you do is very important! What you do makes people happy! The children! Think of the children! It was a people who made you anyway!"

The next morning, very early, a man came along to look at the clock. He opened a door at the back and tinkered with some machinery inside. Soon the duck started laying eggs again. The mouse went in and out. The snake hissed, snatched, and missed.

At eight o'clock, on the hour, the fish began to blow bubbles.

"It was a people who made us!" he said.

"And a people who got us going again!" said the duck.

"Aren't people—" said the mouse, popping out, "*wonderful*!" he said, inside the clock.

"I *don't know*!" hissed the snake. "I don't know!"

مِیرا نام ہے جہانگیر

Copy-Cat Friends

by Pratima Mitchell

Davey was six and a half and so was
Jonny. They were best friends, and because
their birthdays were only three weeks apart
they thought of themselves almost as twins.
They lived next door to each other and
their mothers were also friends. Davey's
mother was born and brought up near
Norwich and Jonny's in Lahore, Pakistan.
Davey's name was a shorter form of David.
Jonny's real name was Jehangir, which
means "Ruler of the World". His big sister,

Razia, said that it suited him perfectly since he seemed to get his own way most of the time.

Perhaps because Davey was a few weeks older than Jonny, he managed to keep half a step ahead of him in learning new things. He learnt to walk and talk and to read and ride his bike just a little before Jonny did. And Jonny was always keen on following Davey. He had to have the same kind of shoes with a Velcro fastening, which made a tearing noise when you tugged at it, the same kind of blue and red anorak and the same toys that Davey had. Jonny even secretly wished that his mother would exchange her salwar-kameez for the short dresses that Mrs Hobson wore. He wished she would go into the swimming pool with him and Davey. He wished she would cook things like Yorkshire pudding and jam roly-poly which he loved to eat at Davey's. And when, shortly after his sixth birthday, his parents arranged for him to begin learning Urdu (their own language) he wouldn't go to classes. Davey didn't learn Urdu, so why should he?

His father found this all rather amusing and called him "my little English boy", but Razia was irritated by it and thought their parents were spoiling him. "You're a copy-cat, Jehangir Ahmad," she would tell him, "and you know what happens to copy-cats. They get eaten by *tigers*." She bared her teeth and growled.

Davey's mother thought Jonny was lovely. She took the boys for walks, one on each side, and called them her twins. "Look," she told her friends and relations, "one blond and one dark. Inseparable they are, too, a proper David and Jonathan."

One day in the spring term a new craze swept Capel Cross First School. Davey and Jonny's teacher, young and energetic Miss Pinkerton, persuaded the Head (middle-aged and a trifle dusty) that writing letters was the best, if not the only, way to get the children's work going. Miss Pinkerton was becoming a little bored with their diaries.

All the children seemed to do the same things every Saturday – watching television and shopping.

"We could set up a postbox, a sorting office and a post office in the Hall," said Miss Pinkerton enthusiastically. "We'd get ever such good value from one project – maths and reading and language games." She looked so keen that the Head gave in.

The first week of the letter-writing project had letters flying in all directions. The Juniors wrote to the Infants, the Infants wrote to Top Juniors and everyone wrote to the cook or the lollipop lady. Davey wrote a letter to the caretaker.

"Hey, Mum," he chatted on the way home from school, "guess what I wrote to Mr Ogg? Dear Mr Ogg, thank you for cleaning the bog." And he and Jonny creased themselves laughing.

"Who's written to the two of you, then?" asked Mrs Hobson.

"I had a letter from Davey," said Jonny.

"I had one from Jonny," said Davey.

"I wrote to the Queen and Miss Pinkerton," said Jonny.

"I bet they won't write back, will they?" said Davey.

"Tell you what, Davey," said his mum, "I'll write you a letter. And I'll ask your mum to write to you, Jonny. We'll put a letter in your lunch-boxes every day."

Next day, at lunch-time, Davey opened his lunch-box. Cheese and tomato sandwich, Hula-hoops and a Penguin. There was something else in there, too – a letter. He opened the envelope, took it out and read aloud. "Dear Davey, I hope you are having a good time. Please finish your s-s-oh yes, sandwich. Bring home the crumbs for me to eat. See you. Love, Goldie." He looked excitedly round the table. "My goldfish wrote to me!"

Jonny opened his lunch-box. Jam sandwich, crisps and an apple. He had a letter as well. He smoothed it out on the crumby, sticky table. "Hello, Jonny, Love Amma", he read.

From then on a note appeared every day in their lunch-boxes except once, when

Mrs Hobson had a doctor's appointment, and once when Mrs Ahmad had to leave early in the morning, to look for new curtain material at the open-air market.

Sometimes Mrs Hobson wrote funny letters.

"Davey Hobson, your hair is like toffee, and I know that your ears are full of milky coffee."

Jonny always got the same letter, "Hello Jonny," or "Hello Jehangir, Love Amma."

"Your mum isn't good at writing funny letters, is she?" observed Sally, who was reading over Jonny's shoulder.

Jonny didn't answer. He knew that his mother had gone to school in Pakistan and that she had been taught in Urdu, the language of Pakistan. She was learning to read and write in English with her friend Mrs Adams but it took a long time to learn a new language.

Jonny went home and complained. "Your letters are so boring," he told his mother. "Everyone laughs when Davey reads his mum's letters."

"If that's how you feel, I shan't bother writing at all," said his mother crossly.

Jonny felt bad about being rude to his mother. He nestled his chin on her lap where she sat knitting a sweater. "Write to me in Urdu, Amma," he said, trying to win favour with her again. "Then you'll be able to say all kinds of things."

The next day at lunch-time Jonny unfolded his mum's letter. She had written beautiful, flowing Urdu letters which looked like flowering grasses and stars and raindrops showering on a window pane.

"Dear Jonny," he pretended to read because he couldn't read a single word in Urdu. "What's yellow and goes Slam! Slam! Slam!" He looked at his friends sitting round the table. "A banana closing a door!"

The joke went down a treat, but Samina snatched the letter from Jonny's hand and read it for herself.

"It doesn't say that," she shouted triumphantly. "It's in Urdu and you can't read Urdu. It says 'Dear Jonny, Don't forget we are going to have tea with Aunty Rashida. Come home straight after school, Love, Amma.' "

That weekend Jonny asked his mother to teach him Urdu. She bought him a blue exercise book with blank, unlined pages and a fountain pen. "It's better to use a proper ink pen with a nib," she explained. First he learned to write his own name, starting from the right hand side of the page and going across to the left. Then when he could do that easily she made him copy a sentence, My name is Jehangir. She made him trace it over her own writing until he could write it on his own from memory.

By the end of the summer term Jonny was reading and writing easy sentences on his own. At school, the letter-writing craze had given way to a school newspaper, but Jonny continued to get letters from his mother in his lunch-box; not every day, but quite often. They were written in Urdu and he could now read them, which he did, softly, to himself. He didn't want Samina

Ashraf making fun of him in front of all the others.

Now it was Davey who felt left out. He and Jonny had always done everything together, but he couldn't share Jonny's letters.

There was only one thing to do. The next Saturday morning he climbed over the wall into Jonny's garden where Mrs Ahmad was hanging out the washing.

"Aunty Firoza," he began, addressing her in the way she preferred, "Will you teach me your language? I like the curly letters and I want to write with a real pen. Then I'll be able to read Jonny's letters and we can play spies and send each other secret messages. Will you teach me in the holidays?"

Mrs Ahmad smiled at him. "Of course I'll teach you, Davey. After all, you and Jonny are meant to be twins, aren't you? Let's start now. Say *Challo* – that means 'Come on'." She patted him on the head and, picking up her laundry basket, led the way indoors.

Fair Donald, Dark Donald

by Judith O'Neill

Long, long ago, on the Isle of Skye, there once lived two brothers. They were fishermen and, although they were brothers, they both had the same name – Donald. The older brother was called Fair Donald and the younger brother was called Dark Donald. Fair Donald had hair so fair it was almost white. Dark Donald had hair so dark it was almost black.

Fair Donald and Dark Donald lived with their old father in a little low house near the shore of a great sea loch. The house was made from big grey stones. The roof was made from grassy turfs. Inside the house there was only one room. The fire was on a stone hearth in the very middle of the room and the smoke crept out through a hole in the roof, just over the fire.

The old father had once been a fisherman too, but now his strength was gone. He stayed at home and looked after the cow who lived inside the house all through the cold winter. He kept a good peat fire burning on the hearth. He made thick potato soup in a black pot over the fire and he baked flat oatcakes on a griddle.

Early in the morning, whenever the weather was calm, just as it was getting light, Fair Donald and Dark Donald rowed their fishing boat far out on the green waters of the great sea loch. They let down their nets. They sat quietly in the boat and waited for hours and hours. Then they pulled the heavy nets, full of shining fish, back into the boat. Fair Donald and Dark Donald rowed back to the white sandy beach. They packed their fish into two wicker baskets. With the baskets on their backs, the two brothers walked three miles along the shore to the nearest village. In the village a boatman bought all their fish and took it over the sea to sell to the people who lived on the mainland.

When their wicker baskets were empty, Fair Donald and Dark Donald walked the three miles back home again. They were tired now, and hungry. It was almost night-time. Their father always had the big pot of soup waiting for them and flat oatcakes on the griddle. As soon as they got home, the two brothers sat down with their father close to the warm peat fire in the middle of the room and ate their supper. Every evening, winter and summer, not long after the sun had set, Fair Donald climbed into his bed tucked away in the west wall. Dark Donald climbed into his bed tucked away in the south wall. The old father climbed into his bed tucked away on the east wall. The cow lay down near the door by the north wall. Soon they were all fast asleep.

Very early the next morning, just as it was getting light, the two brothers woke up. They ate their breakfast of thick white porridge with fresh milk from the cow and they rowed far out on the green waters of the great sea loch.

One dark winter's evening, as Fair Donald and Dark Donald and their old father were eating their supper by the fire, a sudden storm came rolling in across the loch. Lightning flashed, thunder roared, the wind howled round the house and the rain came pelting down. Out on the loch the waves rose higher and higher. On sand and rock the salt water crashed and foamed.

"What a terrible storm!" cried Fair Donald, raising his voice above the noise of wind and waves and rain. He pulled his stool up closer to the fire.

"I'm glad we're not out on the loch tonight," said Dark Donald. "Our boat would be smashed to smithereens!"

The little stone house seemed to shake

as the wind tore wildly at the turfs on the roof and the rain beat hard against the walls.

Suddenly Fair Donald lifted up his head.

"Listen!" he said. "Do you hear that sound?"

"I can hear the wind and the rain," said Dark Donald.

"I can hear the thunder and the waves on the rocks," said the old father.

"No, no! That's not the sound I mean! Listen!"

All three of them sat in silence and listened. Very, very faintly, they heard a little cry, almost drowned by the roar of the storm.

"Miaow! Miaow! Miaow!"

"It's a cat!" cried Dark Donald. "A cat out in the storm!"

"Let her in! Let her in!" cried the old father. "We can't leave a poor cat to wander about on a night like this!"

Fair Donald went to the door and opened it just a narrow crack. He peered out into the darkness. The icy wind whipped against his face. There on the stone step sat a small black cat, wet and shivering in the cold, mewing sadly over and over again.

"Miaow! Miaow! Miaow!" she said.

"Come in, come in, little cat!" cried Fair Donald, and he opened the door a bit wider.

The little black cat walked in through the door and went across at once to the fire. Water streamed down from her black fur and ran into a pool on the floor.

"You poor wee thing!" said Dark Donald.

He took down his towel from its hook on the wall and he rubbed the cat's wet fur until it was dry.

"Sit here by the fire, little cat," he said, "and we'll bring you some milk in a dish."

Fair Donald warmed the milk in the pot. He took his own dish down from its shelf on the wall and he filled it almost to the brim. He broke up an oatcake and he stirred the pieces into the milk. Then he put the dish down on the hearth.

"Drink up! Drink up, little cat!" he said gently. "You must stay by our fire till the storm is gone."

The little black cat lapped and lapped at the milk. She purred as she drank. Soon the dish was clean. The little black cat washed her face and her paws. She curled up in a ball on the hearth. She closed her eyes and fell fast asleep.

"Sssh! Sssh!" whispered Dark Donald. "We mustn't wake her!"

He blew out the candle. Fair Donald, Dark Donald and the old father crept quietly into their beds. All night long the storm raged and howled round the low stone house but the little black cat did not stir.

Very early the next morning, just as it was getting light, Fair Donald and Dark Donald woke up. The storm was over. They climbed down from their beds. There on the hearth was the little black cat, still fast asleep. The old father got out of bed and he set up the smouldering peat on the fire to make it burn more brightly. He milked the cow. The big pot of porridge had been cooking all night on the hearth. Soon it was ready for breakfast.

Now the little black cat began to stir. She opened her eyes and looked carefully all round the room. She stood up and stretched herself. She washed her face and her paws.

"You must have some of our porridge before you go," said Dark Donald, "and some fresh creamy milk from our cow." He took down his dish from the shelf. He filled the dish with thick white porridge from the pot and he poured on fresh milk from a jug. He put the dish down on the hearth.

"Eat up! Eat up, little cat!" he said gently.

The little black cat lapped and lapped at the porridge. She purred as she ate. When the dish was clean, she walked across the room and stood by the door.

"She wants to go out!" said the old father.

Fair Donald opened the door. The winter sun was shining. The sky was clear and the waters of the loch were calm.

"Miaow!" cried the little black cat, and she ran out of the door.

"Where is she going?" asked Dark Donald.

"Where did she come from?" asked Fair Donald.

The two brothers stood with their father on the stone step. They watched the little black cat running across the heather towards the hills. They watched her till she was out of sight.

"We must get ready for the fishing," said Fair Donald.

The two brothers ate up their porridge and milk. Then Dark Donald gathered the nets in his arms. They walked down to the white sand. They dragged their boat over the sand right to the water's edge and they rowed far out on the green waters of the great sea loch.

Winter ended at last. Spring came to the

Isle of Skye with wild flowers along the shore and birds' nests in the heather. Spring turned to summer, to long warm days and clear starry nights. As autumn came on, the heather turned slowly from purple to brown and the days grew shorter and colder. Early in the morning, whenever the weather was calm, just as it was getting light, Fair Donald and Dark Donald set out in their boat for the day's fishing. And in the evening, when the fish had been sold, they came home to a good pot of soup and a flat oatcake and a warm peat fire on the hearth.

One misty day in November, when the two brothers were fishing far out in the middle of the loch, a sharp cold wind began to blow from the north. A sheet of bright lightning flashed across the sky and thunder rolled in the distance.

"There's a bad storm coming!" cried Dark Donald.

"Let's pull in the nets and turn for home!" cried Fair Donald.

Their nets were still empty but they

pulled them in. They grabbed the oars and began to row hard towards the shore. The wind blew louder and stronger. The rain poured down in torrents. The waves surged higher and higher. The little boat was tossed this way and that. Water poured over her sides. The brothers rowed and rowed with all their strength but the wind and the tide kept dragging them back. Night began to come on. Still the storm raged and howled. For the first time in their lives, the two brothers felt frightened.

"What can we do?" shouted Fair Donald over the noise of the wind and the waves.

"We're sure to drown!" Dark Donald shouted back, gripping his oars in terror.

The little boat was lifted up, up, up on the huge white waves and flung down, down, down into the black hollows between the waves. The wind was blowing her further and further from home. The tide was pulling her nearer and nearer to the rocky shore on the far side of the loch.

"The boat is sinking!" called Fair Donald.

"We'll be smashed against the rocks!" shouted Dark Donald.

"There's no hope left!" cried Fair Donald.

The two brothers clung to each other as the little boat pitched and tossed and rolled in the stormy sea. They were drenched to the skin. They were shaking with fear and with cold.

"Help! Help!" they called in despair, but there was no one to hear them.

Suddenly an enormous wave seized their boat and flung it on the rocks. The boat was smashed to smithereens. Fair Donald and Dark Donald were bleeding and bruised, but somehow they were still alive. Slowly, very slowly, they crawled in the dark over the rocks and away from the loch. They slipped on the slime and they cut themselves on the jagged stones. At last they reached a beach of soft white sand. They lay there, groaning with cold and with pain.

Fair Donald lifted up his head and looked around him. He could see nothing at all. The night was pitch black and the

storm was still raging. Slowly, very slowly, he dragged himself to his feet. Again he looked all around him. Far, far in the distance, across the wet heather, he saw a faint light.

"Look!" he cried. "A light! Someone must live there!"

Dark Donald was still lying on the sand. He could hardly lift his head.

"But no one lives on this side of the loch," he said. "There's not a house for miles!"

"Where there's a light, there must be a house," said Fair Donald. "And where there's a house, there must be a fire and food. Come on! We must go and see."

Fair Donald took his brother's hands and pulled him to his feet. Together they limped and stumbled over the rough heather towards the shining light.

As they came nearer and nearer to the light, they saw that it shone from the window of a tiny stone house. They felt their way to the door. They knocked on the door and waited. Slowly, very slowly, the door opened just a narrow crack.

"Who's there?" asked a strange, frightened voice.

"We're two fishermen wrecked in the storm," said Fair Donald.

"Can you please give us shelter for the night?" asked Dark Donald.

The door opened a little bit wider. Now the brothers could see the wrinkled face of an old, old woman. She had a long black shawl over her head. She held a flickering candle in her hand.

"What are your names, fishermen?" she asked, peering out at them. "And where do you come from?"

"We are brothers," said Fair Donald. "Our names are Fair Donald and Dark Donald. We live with our old father on the other side of the loch. Please let us in. We will do you no harm. All we want is shelter for the night."

Now the old woman opened her door wide.

"Fair Donald and Dark Donald!" she cried. "Come in! Come in! I've a nice pot of soup on the fire and a good piece of oatcake on the griddle. I've a wide bed in the wall where you can sleep all night and two fine black sheepskins to keep you warm. Come in, come in, and sit by my fire!"

Fair Donald and Dark Donald walked into the tiny room. A bright peat fire was burning on the hearth. The water poured down from their heavy wet clothes and ran into pools on the hard earth floor.

"Here is a towel!" cried the old woman as she lifted it down from a hook on the wall. "Take off your wet clothes and rub yourselves dry. And here is some ointment that I made from wild herbs. Rub it into your cuts and soon they will heal."

Fair Donald and Dark Donald did all that the old woman said. Soon they were warm and dry. Their pains had gone. They wrapped themselves up in the fine black sheepskins and sat down close to the fire.

The old woman brought them soup and oatcake. The two brothers were so tired they could hardly speak to thank her. They ate up the soup with wooden spoons. They ate up every morsel of the oatcake. Then they slowly climbed into the bed in the wall. They pulled the sheepskins up over their bodies. Just before they closed their eyes, they saw the old woman wringing the water from their clothes and spreading them out by the fire to dry.

When they woke up in the morning, the door of the tiny house stood open and pale winter sunshine streamed into the room. The storm was over. The rain had stopped. A blackbird was singing in the heather. The old woman was standing by her fire. She was stirring and stirring at a big pot of porridge. Fair Donald and Dark Donald could see her better now. Her hands were gnarled and crooked. Her back was humped and bent. Under the black shawl that covered her head, her hair hung down, long and grey. She was a strange, strange old woman, but her face had a kindly smile.

"Your clothes are dry now, Fair Donald," she said gently. "Here they are, all ready for you. And here are your clothes,

Dark Donald, dry as a bone and warm from a night by the fire. Your porridge is almost cooked. Time to be up now. The sun is shining. You'll have a long walk round the top of the loch to get home to your father's house. He'll be thinking the two of you were drowned in the storm last night. How glad he'll be to see you walking in at the door, alive and well after all!"

Soon the two brothers were up and dressed in their own warm clothes again. They sat by the fire and ate the thick white porridge. When at last they were finished, Fair Donald spoke to the old woman.

"How can we thank you for all your kindness?" he said. "You have taken us in from the storm and given us food and fire and bed. You have welcomed us here like your own sons!"

"You must let us pay you something for all you have done," said Dark Donald. "We have no money with us here but back in our father's house we have two silver coins hidden away behind a stone in the wall. We'll walk home now round the top of the loch and we'll take our two silver coins and we'll bring them straight back to you before the sun goes down."

The old woman laughed a strange, long laugh and she smiled at the two brothers by the fire.

"No, no, no!" she said. "I don't want your two silver coins. Keep them to buy yourselves a new boat. You have no need to thank me at all. You were kind to me so I was kind to you. You took me in from the storm. You gave me food and fire and bed. You did me no harm when I came to your door so I did you no harm when you came to mine."

Fair Donald and Dark Donald stared at the old woman in astonishment.

"But we've never seen you in our lives before!" cried Fair Donald. "You've never come knocking at our door!"

"No, indeed, you have not!" cried Dark Donald. "We've never set eyes on you before!"

"Don't you remember a little black cat, wet and shivering in the rain?" asked the old woman, smiling.

Fair Donald and Dark Donald nodded their heads.

"Yes, we remember," they said together.

"And you took her in and you gave her food and she slept all the night on your hearth by the fire?"

"Yes, we remember," they said again.

"I am the Witch-Cat!" cried the old woman and she hobbled quickly out through the door.

Fair Donald and Dark Donald hurried after her but she was nowhere to be seen. They stood together on the stone step and looked out across the heather towards the hills. Far, far in the distance they thought they could see a little black cat, running and leaping in the sunshine. Slowly, very slowly, the two brothers set out on their long walk home.

Tea at
Mrs Manderby's

by Adèle Geras

". . . twenty-two, twenty-three, twenty-four, twenty-five. There!" Hannah smiled at the pennies she'd been counting: this week's pocket money, and a few pennies from last week's, and the rest from the transparent plastic pig in which she kept her savings. She pushed them in a long line across the table, and then began to pile them into shaky brown towers.

"Let's go to the shop now, Dad," she said, but Dad was washing plates noisily in the sink, and not paying attention. "Dad?"

"What?"

"I said, may we go to the shop now?"

"Which shop is that?"

"The junk shop," said Hannah.

"What for?"

"To buy something."

"I don't know what Mum'll say. We've got a whole house full of junk, quite a lot of it in your room, too. Why do you want to spend good pocket money on it?"

"It's not junk I want to buy. It's a doll. I saw it there last week."

"It's probably been sold, then," said Dad, swooshing fluffy soapsuds down into the plughole with his hands.

"No it hasn't." Hannah smiled.

"How do you know?"

"Because I asked Mr Spatten to keep it for me, and he said he would, if I paid him some money as a deposit. He explained all about it. You pay some money, and it means that something is a bit yours, but not enough to take away. Then you go and pay the rest of the money, and after that what you want is all yours and you can take it home."

"Where did you get the money from?" Dad asked.

"I saved it."

"I see. Well, all right then, if you let me drink my coffee in peace, and give me half an hour to read the paper, then we'll go down to the junk shop together. OK?"

"OK," said Hannah. "There are things I have to do, anyway."

Dad was already reading. From time to time, his hand crept out round the side of the newspaper, and waved over the table, like a slow, five-headed creature with bad eyesight, looking for the cup. Hannah put the money into her pencil case and went upstairs.

In her room, she dropped each penny carefully into her purse, and then she put the purse into her best red handbag. "You lot," she said to the row of plump, well-dressed dolls lined up on the shelf, "are going to have a big surprise today." Hannah waited for the dolls to take in this news, and then went on: "Yes, I'm bringing home a friend for you, and you are all to be nice to her. I won't have any rude remarks about how shabby she is, and you're to have her to all your tea parties." Ruby Tuesday, the brown velvet rag doll, had a doubtful look in her eye. "Ruby," said Hannah, "she's really lovely. She was in a big box when I found her. How would you like to lie in a cardboard box full of broken saucers, and cracked photograph frames, and old plastic egg-cups and dirty shoes? I had to rescue her, didn't I?" Dolly Daydream's pink, turned-up nose turned up even higher, it seemed to Hannah. "Dolly," she said, "I shall clean her up, don't you worry, and then I dare say she'll be as pretty as you. Prettier, even." All the dolls made round eyes, full of amazement. Dolly Daydream was the most expensive of them all, and the biggest. Hannah thought she was stuck up and not a bit cuddly, with cold, pink hands and feet and fat, smug cheeks. "Jenny, you'll look after her, I know, because you're so kind." Jenny had been loved to tatters since Hannah was a baby, but her bright red smile was still neatly stitched to her cotton face, and what was left of her brown wool hair was tidily parted in the middle. "What shall we call her?" Hannah asked the dolls. Ruby, Dolly Daydream, Jenny, Little Sadie, Skinny Lizzy and all the others said nothing. Hannah said: "Well, you're a lot of help, I must say. I shall think of a name all by myself." She thought for a moment. "The new doll will be called Belle. I've just de-cided." This was not quite true. Belle had been the name of the doll in the junk shop for a whole week, ever since Hannah had pulled her out of the rubbish box. It suited her perfectly.

"Hannah!" shouted Dad from down-stairs, "are you coming, then? We have to be back before Mum gets home from the library. We're going to tea at Mrs Manderby's, remember?"

"Coming, Dad," said Hannah, and felt herself turning cross and sad all over. Why did today, her special, Belle-buying day, have to be spoiled by tea at Mrs Manderby's? Hannah could never understand why they had to go. On the way to the shop, she asked: "Why do we go there? I hate her."

"Don't say that, Hannah. It's not kind and it's not true. Mrs Manderby is a lonely old lady, who doesn't have a great deal of fun in her life. She looks forward to seeing us. It's a treat for her."

"Then why is she so cross? Why does she never smile? Why do I have to sit still and keep quiet? Why can't I touch things in her house? Why is it so dark and stuffy in her lounge? Why doesn't she let me have more than two biscuits? Why can't I go there in my jeans?"

"Gosh!" said Dad. "Is this some kind of quiz show? I've never heard so many questions in all my life. One answer for all of them, really."

"What is it?"

"When Mrs Manderby was a girl, the world was very different. No television, very few cars or aeroplanes. People had different ideas then about how children should behave and dress, and Mrs Manderby is simply treating you in the way that she was treated when she was a child."

"I don't believe she ever was a child," said Hannah.

"Of course she was, love. Everyone was a child once."

"But she's so thin and pointed and black and straight, I just can't see her as a child. I think she was always just like she is now."

"Come on," said Dad. "Forget about Mrs Manderby for a while and let's go and fetch that doll."

Hannah and her father went into the junk shop, and Hannah wondered for the hundredth time why the treasures that stood heaped on shelves and in boxes and on the floor were called "junk". Who had decided that a plate with a picture of floating blue ribbons and pink roses should be thrown out? Why did the owner of the china cups with dragons curling round the edges not like them enough to keep them? Didn't people collect postcards any more? There were boxes of old, brown, picture postcards with spidery, forgotten handwriting on the back – did nobody want to remember holidays and journeys? Hannah loved everything in the shop, everything that was no more use to anyone.

"I'm going to see what I can find," said Dad. He enjoyed the junk shop as much as Hannah, although his treasures were of a different kind: records with torn covers, books with gold writing on the spine, and little, black letters squeezed together into lines. Hannah went up to Mr Spatten, who was standing behind a counter full of old lamps, candlesticks and mountains of white plates.

"Good afternoon, Mr Spatten," she said politely.

"Ah," said Mr Spatten, pushing his glasses into a better position on his nose, and wiping his feathery moustache with a spotted handkerchief. "Miss Hannah, is it? Yes? Are you well? Are you happy? Do you see anything your heart desires or your house requires?"

"I can't see it, Mr Spatten, what my heart desires, I mean, but I know you've kept it for me." Mr Spatten looked puzzled. "The doll," Hannah said quickly. "You said you'd keep her for me. I found her in that box over there. I paid you a deposit of one penny. You said you'd keep her for me."

"Ah . . . a deposit, now, is it? Bless my little cotton socks, you're going to be a banker when you grow up. Who told you about deposits?"

"You did, Mr Spatten." Hannah's voice remained polite, but her heart was bumping about so loudly that she could hear it in her head. Had Mr Spatten forgotten? Had he sold the doll? Hannah gulped. "You put her into a drawer. You promised to look after her."

"I'm sure you're right, child. Let's have a shufti."

"What's that? I don't want a shufti. I want my doll." Tears were winking in

Hannah's eyes, fighting to come out. She blinked them away.

Mr Spatten said: "A shufti means a look. Let's have a look is what I meant. This one first, I think." He picked at things in a jumbled drawer, and said "Amazing what you find, isn't it? When you visit a drawer after a long time. Only a messy one, mind. No adventures in a tidy drawer, are there?"

He found the doll at last, half-hidden under a felt hat with holes in the brim. "There she is!" shouted Hannah. "There's Belle!"

"Aha! I see now why you were so anxious to find her," said Mr Spatten. "In bad condition, and no clothes to speak of, but yes, a beauty. A china-headed doll, with a stuffed leather body, dating from about 1900. An old doll indeed. And how much am I charging for this treasure?"

"You said 25p," said Hannah, taking out her purse.

"I'm a fool," said Mr Spatten, "but there you are. I think I shall put the price up . . ." (a tear plopped from Hannah's eye and puddled on to the dusty glass of the counter) ". . . to 25p and a big, happy smile from you, my girl."

"Oh, thank you," said Hannah, and smiled till her cheeks hurt. She poured the twenty-five pence on to the counter and took Belle into her arms. "There's one back for you, you know," said Mr Spatten. "Don't forget you've already paid one penny as a deposit." Hannah took it.

"Goodbye, Mr Spatten," she said. "Thank you so much."

When Hannah and her father arrived home, Mum was waiting. She worked as a librarian, and always finished early on Saturdays. After she had admired Belle for five whole minutes, she sent Hannah upstairs to change into a dress. The time had come for tea at Mrs Manderby's. Hannah said to Belle: "You can come too, Belle. I won't mind so much if you're there. I shall sit on my chair and hold you on my lap. I don't care how sour Mrs Manderby looks, I shall talk to you, that's all."

The Blaines's house and Mrs Manderby's house were in the same street, and it took exactly sixty seconds to cross the road and travel back in time over fifty years. The strangeness began in the garden. Every other garden in the street had roses in the summer, daffodils and crocuses clumped together in the spring, and rhododendrons that looked good enough to eat: sugar pink, and pale mauve and white. Some hedges were neat, others untidy. Some drives were swept clean, others were dotted with leaves, crisp bags, and old notes written to the milkman. But in Mrs Manderby's garden flowers did what they were told, and lived in round, neatly-made beds cut into the grass. The lawn always looked as if it had just been brushed and combed. Not a single leaf stuck out from the flat surface of the hedge, and there was not a crisp bag in the whole world brave enough to blow on to Mrs Manderby's drive.

Dad knocked at the door, and Hannah heard the tapping of the old lady's stick on the wooden floor. The first thing, thought Hannah, was to get safely past the tiger skin stretched out in the hall. It was only the skin of a tiger, but Hannah didn't like the way the head stuck up, and she hated the amber glass eyes and the yellowing teeth. She clutched Belle under one arm, and hung on to her mother's hand.

"My dears." Mrs Manderby had opened the door. "How very kind of you to call. Do come in. How do you do, Hannah?"

"How do you do, Mrs Manderby?" Hannah answered politely. The first time Mrs Manderby had asked her how she did, Hannah had said: "I'm fine, thank you," and Mrs Manderby had spent the rest of the afternoon talking about the absence of good manners in the world today. It still seemed silly to Hannah to answer one question with another, and she thought that people only did it when they couldn't think of anything interesting to talk about.

· Dad held the door open while the ladies (which included Hannah) followed Mrs Manderby into the room which Hannah called the lounge, and Mrs Manderby called the drawing room. Hannah sat on the chair with a tapestry seat which made her legs itch. If only she could have worn her jeans. Dad and Mum sat on a funny kind of sofa with no arms and only half a back, which was called a *chaise longue*. This, Hannah had been told, meant "long chair" in French. Mrs Manderby sat in a brown leather chair with fat armrests. The room looked dark, even though the sun was shining. Maybe it was the maroon wallpaper and the almost-black wood of the table. Hannah shut her ears to the quiet talk of the grown-ups and chatted to Belle in her head: "Isn't it awful, not being able to touch? Look at that box. I bet it's a musical box. Can you see the apple tree in the back garden? Maybe I'll ask to go out after tea. Mrs Manderby's husband shot the tiger in India, a long time ago. That's him over there. Doesn't he look funny in that hat? Mrs Manderby hasn't any children. I wonder what she does when we're not here? I wonder what upstairs is like . . .?" Mrs Manderby's voice pulled Hannah out of her thoughts.

". . . like a biscuit, my dear?"

"Yes, please," said Hannah, and stood up to take one. As she did so, Belle fell off her lap and flopped on to the carpet, taking with her the teacup that had been balanced on a little table next to Hannah's chair. A brown stain crept and spread over the carpet. Hannah looked at her parents, and trembled. Dad said: "Never mind, love," Mum said: "Don't worry, I'll get a cloth," and Hannah said: "I'm terribly sorry," all at the same time. They all waited for Mrs Manderby's anger. But Mrs Manderby wasn't listening. She had picked Belle up, and was sitting with the old doll in her lap, turning her over and over, fingering the torn lace of her dress, and stroking her smooth, hard cheek. Mrs Manderby's eyes shone with tears as she stared at Belle. She took a handkerchief out of her pocket and wiped them. Hannah could not understand why the old lady was so upset. She prayed for an earthquake or a flood: something that would make Mrs Manderby forget about the carpet.

It was an accident. Everyone spilled cups of things by mistake. She thought of her father's hand, waving above the coffee cup at lunch-time. Why, then, was Mrs Manderby crying? Hannah supposed she must love the carpet. She said: "Don't worry, Mrs Manderby. We can send the carpet to the cleaners. It'll come back good as new, really. I'm ever so sorry." Mrs Manderby looked up and laughed through her tears. Hannah had never seen her laugh before.

"Silly goose! Do you think I'm crying about a carpet? Why, I spill things myself, nearly every day, although in my case the cause is arthritis in my fingers."

"Then why are you crying?"

"Because I've just seen someone I loved very much a long time ago, and she hasn't changed, and I have, and it makes me feel sad."

"There's no one here except us," said Hannah.

"There's Clara," said Mrs Manderby.

"Who's she?"

"The doll," said Mrs Manderby, and held Belle's face next to her cheek.

"She's mine," said Hannah. "I bought her today in the junk shop."

"And I'm glad you did. I gave her away to my godchild fifty years ago, when we left for India, and I haven't seen her since then. My lovely Clara, how battered and how miserable you look, but how beautiful, still." Mrs Manderby handed the doll back to Hannah. "I'm sure you will take care of her, and never give her away."

"I won't," said Hannah, "not even if I go to India when I'm grown up."

"Perhaps we could make her a new dress." The old lady's eyes shone. "You must come tomorrow, Hannah, and help me sort out the trunks upstairs. All my old evening gowns are there, and my fans. We could make her a few very pretty frocks. Would you like that?"

"I'd love it. I'll come tomorrow. Would you like to see my other dolls?"

"Certainly. We'll have a tea party under the apple tree. All your dolls are cordially invited."

Hannah grinned. "They all cordially accept," she said.

It was time to go home. As they stood at the door, Hannah saw her father and Mrs Manderby whispering together. Then he bounded up the stairs and came down holding an old photograph with curled-over edges. He gave it to Hannah. Mrs Manderby said: "That's me, aged five. And that's Clara."

Hannah looked. A fat little girl, dressed in a frilly white pinafore and high-buttoned boots, stared at her from under a curly fringe of black hair. In her hand was Belle, dressed in lace and ribbons. Hannah put the photograph into Mrs Manderby's hand. She said: "You're both the same now, really, only older. I shall call Belle Clarabelle, because she *is* yours, still, as well as mine. Is Clarabelle a good name?"

"An excellent name," said Mrs Manderby. "Very elegant and genteel."

Hannah said: "See you tomorrow", and followed her mother and father down the drive.

The next day, at four o'clock, Hannah and Mrs Manderby sat under the apple tree together. The dolls, all dressed for the party, were lined up on the grass beside a white tablecloth embroidered with flowers and trailing leaves. Clarabelle wore a long blue taffeta skirt made out of an old scarf that Mrs Manderby had found, and she had a square of lace fastened round her shoulders like a shawl.

"I had a beautiful doll's tea-set when I was a girl," said Mrs Manderby. "I wonder what became of it. It would have been such fun to set it out for the dolls this afternoon."

"Never mind," said Hannah. "I think these are lovely." She put a cup and saucer in front of each of the dolls. "They've never had such a grand tea before. Neither have I. Gold-rimmed cups!"

Mrs Manderby had bought cream cakes. There was a plate piled with sandwiches and decorated with frilly lettuce leaves. There were scones with strawberry jam and cream. Mrs Manderby poured tea from a silver teapot with a long curved spout. "Do eat as much as you can, dear," she said.

Hannah did. She ate for herself and for all the dolls. They just sat and smiled in the sunshine that fell through the leaves of the apple tree and made gold spots of light on their pretty dresses.

Macaw and the Blackberry Fishcakes

by John Escott

When Patsy's mum and dad took over Crab Cove's fish and chip shop, they took over Macaw as well.

Patsy, who had always wanted a pet bird, thought Macaw was beautiful with his red, yellow and blue wings and his red breast. Unfortunately, her mother did not think Macaw was quite so lovely.

"I'd have thought twice about coming if I'd known that bird was here," Mrs Forum said. "I'm sure it will cost us a fortune to keep."

Macaw had been left behind by the old owner of the shop because he was going into a rest home and couldn't take his bird with him. Rest homes had strict rules about such things.

"Isn't there a tropical bird garden we can give him to?" Mrs Forum wondered.

"SQUAW!" screamed Macaw.

"I don't think he likes that idea," Mr Forum told his wife.

"Nor do I," said Patsy, pulling a face.

So Macaw stayed, which pleased Patsy very much. And things went quite smoothly until the day of the Crab Cove Hospital Fête . . .

The fête began in the morning and went on all day. Patsy's mum was helping out on Mrs Hatwhistle's stall. Patsy and Macaw had gone along as well.

Macaw was perched in his favourite spot on Patsy's mop of red hair. "YARK!" he shrieked at passers-by, but in a friendly way.

Mrs Hatwhistle's stall was full of goodies. Home-made wine, home-made jam, cakes, biscuits.

"Everything looks lovely, Mrs Hatwhistle," said Patsy.

"HATWHISTLE!" screamed Macaw.

"Really, Patsy!" said Mrs Forum, looking embarrassed. "You must teach that bird some manners."

"Sorry, Mrs Hatwhistle," said Patsy.

"Bless me, dear, I don't mind," laughed Mrs Hatwhistle. "I think Macaw is a scream."

"SCREAM!" screamed Macaw.

"Er – we'll have a look round and come back later," said Patsy.

Now at this time, out in the middle of Crab Bay, there was a large white luxury yacht. It belonged to Mr Hiram J. Beefy, the American beefburger millionaire. He owned burger bars all over America and was shaped a bit like a beefburger himself.

Mr Beefy and his wife, Lydia, were on a world cruise.

"What a darling little place," Mrs Beefy said when she saw Crab Cove. She was as thin as a stick insect, which made people laugh when they heard her married name.

Hiram J. sighed. "Yes, honey." He was bored with cruising. Getting ideas to improve his burger bars was what interested him, and he didn't think Crab Cove would provide him with any of those.

But he was wrong.

Back at the fête, Macaw had taken off from Patsy's hair (which he had got into the habit of using as a landing pad) and flown over to Mrs Hatwhistle's stall again. He seemed especially interested in a bottle of wine that hung in a basket under the canopy of the stall.

"Blackberry Wine – only £1.50" it said on the label.

"SQUAW!" said Macaw – and he picked up the basket by the handle and flew off with it, over the heads of the crowd.

"Macaw!" cried Mrs Forum. "Bring that back at once."

Macaw didn't even look round.

A few minutes later, when Patsy arrived back carrying a large chocolate ice cream, she could see something was wrong by the look on her mother's face.

"Where's Macaw?" she said.

"That *bird*!" shouted Mrs Forum.

In fact, Macaw had taken his prize home. He flew into the kitchen at the back of Forum's Fish Parlour and perched on a shelf above the worktop.

Then, slowly, he pecked the cork from the bottle of wine, the neck hanging over the edge of the shelf . . .

. . . And the wine poured steadily downwards – straight into a large bowl which stood on the worktop. In the bowl was a fishy mixture.

Macaw lost interest in the bottle after the wine had stopped gurgling and he flew out of the window in search of some new adventure.

The fishy mixture gradually changed colour.

Several minutes later, Mr Forum returned to his kitchen after answering the phone. "Now what was I doing?" he said to himself. "Ah, yes. The fishcake mix." And he went over to the large bowl on the worktop and began stirring it. He didn't notice that the fishcake mix had more of a pinky tinge to it now.

Out on Hiram J. Beefy's yacht, the millionaire and his wife were having a late breakfast. Mrs Beefy was eating a grapefruit, while her husband tucked into a king-sized beefburger of the sort that had made him his fortune.

Suddenly, there was a flapping sound, and they both turned to see Macaw landing on the rail of the yacht.

"Look, honey," said Hiram J. "It's a macaw!"

Lydia looked tickled pink. "I wonder if it talks?" she said.

She didn't have to wonder long.

"PIE-AND-CHIPS-CHICKEN-AND-CHIPS
PEA-FRITTERS-FISHCAKES-PASS-THE-

VINEGAR!" screamed Macaw.

Hiram J. stared in astonishment. "Did you hear that, Lydia? He's telling you what is on the menu at some restaurant. Now that's what I call smart. A flying advertisement!"

"WHERE'S-THE-SALT?" shrieked Macaw, and flew off towards Crab Cove.

Hiram J. Beefy forgot about his breakfast. "I have to find out where he's going. I've never tasted a pea-fritter. Who knows, maybe it's something I can introduce into the Burger Bars."

And he called for one of his crew to launch the small boat.

Patsy had arrived back at the shop in time for the midday opening. Because Mrs Forum was staying at the fête, Patsy was to act as waitress at the four tables in Forum's Fish Parlour. But she was worried about Macaw.

Patsy told her father what the bird had done at the fête.

"Dear me," was all that Mr Forum said.

At that moment, Macaw flew past the window and perched on the hanging sign outside the shop.

"There he is!" cried Patsy.

"He's not carrying any bottles of wine," Mr Forum observed.

"Oh dear," said Patsy. "I wonder what he's done with it."

Just then, a large man in expensive yachting clothes came into the shop and collapsed into a chair at one of the tables. He had obviously been running. "Is that . . . your bird?" he gasped, nodding to Macaw outside.

"Er – yes," Patsy admitted, wondering what Macaw had been up to now.

But the man just gave a nod and said, "Good". Without looking at the menu, he said, "I'll have two pea-fritters, two fishcakes and some chips, please."

"Yes, sir," said Patsy, one eye on Macaw.

"YESSIR!" said Macaw through the open window.

The American stayed right through lunchtime. He ate what he had ordered, then he asked Patsy to bring him some more of "those delicious fishcakes".

"He's got an enormous appetite," Patsy whispered to her father.

"It's very strange," said Mr Forum, "but several customers have come back for more fishcakes today. They're all saying how nice they are. It's a good job I made an extra-large helping of mixture."

It was much later, when Patsy was busy clearing up in the kitchen, that she glanced up and saw the empty wine bottle on the shelf.

"So *that's* where it got to," she said. Then she noticed the empty bowl on the worktop beneath it. "Oh, my goodness. Dad!" she called.

Mr Forum came into the kitchen.

"Uh – your fishcakes," she said. "Did you mix them in that?" Patsy nodded to the bowl beneath the empty wine bottle.

"Yes," said Mr Forum. "Why?"

Patsy pointed to the empty wine bottle. "I – er – think you had something extra in today's mix."

Mr Forum looked up at the bottle. "Whatever . . . ?"

"Mrs Hatwhistle's blackberry wine," said Patsy.

"Oh!" said Mr Forum.

Later, when the shop was closing for the afternoon, Hiram J. Beefy went over to the counter to speak to Mr Forum and Patsy.

"Sir," he said. "I'd like to congratulate you on a most original dish."

"You would?" said Mr Forum, looking surprised.

The American nodded. "I'm talking about your fishcakes. I've never tasted any like them before. You must have your own special recipe."

"Well," began Mr Forum.

Hiram J. held up a hand. "Now I don't expect you to tell me your recipe for nothing. What do you say to a thousand dollars?"

Mr Forum blinked in astonishment. Patsy's mouth fell open.

"Oh – well, really – I couldn't—" Mr Forum began.

"Nonsense," said Hiram J. "I insist on paying you something. I want to make and sell them in my Burger Bars in America."

"But – but it was an accident," said Mr Forum.

Now it was Hiram J. Beefy's turn to look surprised. "Accident?"

Mr Forum explained about Macaw and the bottle of wine. "And so what you had this morning," he finished, "were *blackberry* fishcakes. A sort of *freak* fishcake."

Hiram J. began to laugh. "Let's get this straight," he chuckled. "It's a normal fishcake mix, plus one bottle of blackberry wine?" And he laughed and laughed.

Patsy and Mr Forum laughed with him.

In the end, because Mr Forum wouldn't take any money, the millionaire made a generous donation to the hospital fête fund. And Mr Forum told him how to make pea-fritters, free of charge, so Hiram J. Beefy went away a very happy man.

"Wait until we tell Mum," said Patsy, after the American had gone. "She'll have to let Macaw stay now. Blackberry fishcakes could make us millionaires like Mr Beefy."

"Well, we've already sold more than three times the number we usually do," he agreed. "We must tell Mrs Hatwhistle. After all, it was her blackberry wine that did the trick. We'll have to go into business together. The Hatwhistle and Forum Blackberry Fishcake Company!" Mr Forum laughed.

"BLACKBERRY FISHCAKES!" screamed Macaw, automatically adding an extra item to his squawk-aloud menu. "BLACKBERRY FISHCAKES!"

And after that day, they became a regular feature at Forum's Fish Parlour.

The Stonecutter

An Ethiopian Folk Story

Narrated by Gessesse Belay
Retold by Elizabeth Laird

Once upon a time, high up in the mountains of Ethiopia, where buzzards soar about the crags by day, and hyenas roam the plains by night, there lived a poor stonecutter.

Every day, he took his hammer and his chisel, filled his goatskin with water, and set off for the quarry. Every day he listened to the monkeys squabble and chatter in the cliffs above, and watched the painted butterflies hover over the flowers beneath. Every day he toiled under the hot sun, chipping and chopping, hacking and hewing, carving out great stone blocks for the streets and palaces of the wily old Emperor's turreted city.

And then, one day, the wily old Emperor rode by.

Before him trotted a hundred horsemen, and their lion's mane head-dresses fluttered in the breeze. Behind him ran a hundred foot soldiers, and the sun glinted on the polished tips of their spears. A servant held over his head an umbrella of turquoise silk to shield him from the heat, and his mule was covered with a saddle cloth of the richest, softest velvet.

"Oho," said the stonecutter, as he bowed a deep bow to the imperial procession. "That is the life for me. How I wish I was the wily old Emperor!"

The old wizard, who lived deep inside the mountain, heard his wish, and before he could blink his eyes, the stonecutter had been transformed into the Emperor. Dressed in the finest robes, he

was riding the Emperor's own mule, with his horsemen, his foot soldiers and the servant with the turquoise umbrella all in respectful attendance.

"Oh wonderful, marvellous turn of fortune!" said the stonecutter, who was now the Emperor. "Now I am the greatest of all, and everybody will obey me."

For a time, the new Emperor was happy. He granted petitions, punished his enemies, fed his lions, and ate his meals in solemn state behind a curtain.

But one day, the Emperor set out on a journey. The sun rose high in the sky.

"Where is my silk turquoise umbrella?" said the Emperor. "Servants, shade me from the sun!" But his servants had left the umbrella at home.

The Emperor shook his head.

"I am not, after all, the greatest thing in the world," he said. "The sun can make even kings and emperors break out in a sweat, just like an ordinary servant. How I wish I was the sun, high up in the sky!"

The old wizard, who lived deep inside

the mountain, heard his wish, and before he could flick his fly-whisk, the Emperor had become the sun. Burning fiercely, he shone down on the land, and shrivelled up the grass, and dried up the streams and rivers, and made kings and emperors break out in a sweat, just like ordinary servants.

"Oh magical, magnificent fate!" said the Emperor, who was now the sun. "Now I am the greatest of all, and everybody will hide from me."

For a time, the sun was happy. He baked the earth till it cracked, and made the elephants pant for thirst, and dried up the rivers until even the great Nile was no more than a trickle.

But one day, a cloud floated between the sun and the earth.

"My power has gone!" said the sun. "I am not, after all, the greatest thing in the world. This cloud can fill up the streams again, and give the grass new life, and protect the animals and people from my blinding rays. How I wish I was a cloud, pouring water down on the earth, and flooding all the fields, and making people and animals run for their lives!"

The old wizard, who lived deep inside the mountain, heard his wish, and before he could shoot forth another ray, the sun was transformed into a cloud. He floated high above the land, between the earth and the sun.

"Oh splendid, wondrous destiny!" said the sun, who was now a cloud. "Now I am the greatest thing in the world and everybody will fear me."

For a time, the cloud was happy. He poured torrents of water on to the land. Lightning flashed. The river burst its banks, and sheep, cows, donkeys and people were all washed away.

But there was one thing on earth that would not give way before the rushing water. It was a great rock, which stood firm, and the flood was forced to break into two streams to go round it.

"Oh!" said the cloud. "I am not, after all, the greatest thing in the world. Oh how I wish I was a rock! Then nothing on earth would have the power to move me."

The old wizard, who lived deep inside the mountain, heard his wish, and before he could let loose another drop of water, the cloud had become the rock. He stood firm, and felt his mighty strength.

"Oh happy, blessed day!" he said. "Now I am the greatest thing in the world, and everybody will respect me. I will watch the years come and go, and nothing will have the power to touch me."

For a time, the rock was happy. He stood proud and firm, aloft above the plain, and looked down at the people who moved about far below.

But one day, the rock heard a chipping and a chopping, and he felt a hacking and a hewing that shuddered through his marble veins. A stonecutter was hitting at his very roots with his little hammer and chisel.

"Oh," said the rock, "I am not, after all, the greatest thing in the world. Not even I, in my great strength, can stop this busy fellow picking and pecking at my very roots. How I wish I was the stonecutter!"

The old wizard, who lived deep inside the mountain, heard his wish, and before he could send another shower of stones rattling down from his craggy heights, the rock found he had become the stonecutter again, toiling under the hot sun, chipping and chopping, hacking and hewing, to carve out great stone blocks for the streets and palaces of the Emperor's turreted city.

"There is nothing greater than man, and the work of his hands," said the stonecutter, and he laughed long and loud.

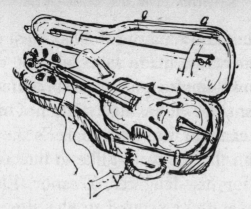

The Little Fiddle

by Eveline de Jong

A long time ago, almost a hundred years or so, many things were different from today. People wore different clothes and there were no cars in the streets. People didn't have radios to listen to, nor did they have televisions to watch. But there was one thing that was just the same as it is today – people enjoyed singing and making music, and they enjoyed listening to other people playing music.

At that time there lived a violin-maker,

who built and repaired violins. Most of the instruments he made were full-size violins for grown-ups to play, but sometimes he made smaller violins for children. One day a man came to the violin-maker's shop and told him that he would like to buy a small violin for his daughter, Eleanor. Eleanor was six and she wanted to play the violin. Of course, she couldn't hold a big instrument, so she needed a small violin to learn on.

The violin-maker set to work and made a beautiful small-size violin for Eleanor. When it was ready, Eleanor and her father came to fetch it. From then on the little fiddle belonged to Eleanor. She practised on it almost every day and soon she was able to play lovely tunes.

Sometimes, when Grandma came to visit, she and Eleanor would make music together: Eleanor on her little fiddle and Grandma on the piano. One day, Uncle Sam also brought his violin, and then all three played a trio together.

Eleanor grew taller, but of course the

little fiddle could not grow with her. In two years Eleanor had become too big to play on the little fiddle. She needed a larger violin so that she could go on learning to play better.

The little fiddle was put away in its case. While it was lying there, it could hear Eleanor practising on her new violin. The little fiddle wished that soon there would be another child who would want to learn to play the violin and for whom it would be just the right size.

The little fiddle didn't have to wait long. One day, some friends came to visit Eleanor and her family. The children, Anna and Christian, were younger than Eleanor. They both liked singing and listening to music and both of them wanted to learn to play the violin. So the little fiddle moved to their house and Anna, who was the eldest, started having violin lessons.

After a while, Anna grew too tall for the little fiddle, but by then Christian was big enough to hold it, so the little fiddle stayed for some more happy years.

After that, for many, many years, the little fiddle lived with different children in a number of different families. Some children were happy to play, others were not. Some children made beautiful sounds and played lovely tunes, others did not.

Once, a boy fell down with the little fiddle and it broke. The boy's mother and father were very cross with him and told him that he should have been more careful. The little fiddle was worried that it was no longer fit to be played. The boy and his mother took the little fiddle to a violin-maker, who repaired the break. The violin-maker also put on a new set of strings, and then the little fiddle was all ready to be played again. All in all, through the ups and downs, the little fiddle had a happy time.

There was, however, just one trace of unhappiness in the little fiddle's life: it sometimes felt a bit lonely. For whenever it played together with other violins, the little fiddle was always the smallest. The little fiddle felt overwhelmed by all the big instruments. Sometimes the little fiddle was not only surrounded by big violins, but also by large voilas, enormous cellos and even a gigantic double bass.

The little fiddle moved house again. This time it went to Vincent. Vincent liked playing the violin, but he didn't like practising. One day the little fiddle was put away in its case, and it was not taken out the following day, or the next day, or the next week. Months went by, a year went by, and still the little fiddle hadn't been taken out of its case. Vincent had stopped playing.

The little fiddle began to lose hope of ever being played again. Its strings broke, first one, then two, and then all the four strings hung loose. Vincent's mother once picked up the case, but only to put it still further away in a cupboard. The family moved house and the little fiddle moved with them, so it had not been completely forgotten, but it did get so badly knocked about that it was broken again.

Time had gone by, and many things

had changed in the world since the little fiddle was made. There were now many cars, buses, and heavy lorries on the roads. People had radios and televisions and computers. Some of the music that people listened to had changed as well, but there were still a lot of people who enjoyed playing the same music and they liked playing it on the instruments that people had used a hundred years ago.

The little fiddle lived in its box, high on a shelf, forlorn and forgotten. Vincent was now grown-up, with a family of his own. One day, a friend came to stay and told him about her little boy called Jacob, who had just started to play the violin. Suddenly, Vincent remembered his own little fiddle.

Immediately he started looking for it all over the house. He found the box, took out the little fiddle and showed it to his friend. The little fiddle looked very pitiful without any strings, and with a break down the side. But, even so, the visitor asked whether she could borrow the little fiddle and take it to a violin-maker so that it could be repaired.

The little fiddle was made whole again. The violin-maker also gave it a fresh coat of varnish and put on new strings. There it was, all new and ready.

The little fiddle was so happy that it could be played once more. It took a bit of time to get used to having strings again and to feeling the bow on its strings. But soon it remembered how to let its body vibrate and how to make beautiful sounds.

The little fiddle now belonged to Jacob. Jacob played his violin at home and at school. The little fiddle was very excited the first time he was taken to school. As soon as it arrived, the little fiddle could hear the sounds of many other violins. Jacob took the little fiddle out of its case, put it under his chin, and joined the other players. It was then that the little fiddle looked round and saw lots of children who were all playing on small violins – some of them even smaller than the little fiddle itself! The little fiddle knew that it would never feel lonely again.

Elena's Story

by Siân Lewis

"You know my new friend, Elena?" Jane asked Miss Jones one March afternoon.

"Yes," smiled Miss Jones.

"She won't talk to me," said Jane. "She's been staying at our house for two whole days now and she's still too shy to say hello. What can I do?"

"Why don't you try reading Elena a story?" Miss Jones asked. "She might like that."

"What a good idea!" said Jane

She knew just the right story for Elena. Miss Jones did too. She fetched the book from the back of the classroom.

"There you are," she said with a smile. "A story specially for Elena. Perhaps when she hears it, she'll talk to you."

Jane rushed off home with the book in her bag. Outside the back door she could hear Elena jumping around in the kitchen. But when she tiptoed to the window and peeped in, Elena stopped.

"Hello!" called Jane with an especially friendly smile on her face.

Elena said nothing.

Jane slipped in through the door.

"Hello," she whispered. "Hello, Elena. Say hello to me."

But Elena ran away. She squeezed herself into the corner between the cupboard and the kitchen wall and crouched there, quiet as a mouse, until Jane's big face came and found her.

"Hello," Jane said, right at her.

Elena closed her eyes tight.

"Come on. Talk to me," whispered Jane.

"Don't be shy. Look what I've got. A book! I'm going to read you a story."

Elena heard the jingle of a satchel and peeped out very carefully. What she saw was the sun spinning in through the kitchen window and skipping on the book in Jane's hand. The pictures on the book danced like new leaves on the trees. Elena opened her eyes wide.

"Hello," said Jane at once. "Hello, Elena. Hell-o-o!"

At the third hello Elena shuffled her feet.

"Hello," said Jane for the fourth time.

"Yuk!" said Elena loudly.

"You're talking!" Jane cheered. "Good old Elena!" Her face came right into the gap between the cupboard and the wall. "Come on," she said excitedly. "Say hello to me. Hell-o."

"Yuk!" spat Elena.

And that's all she would say, no matter how much Jane coaxed her.

"All right, then," sighed Jane. "I'll read you a story, but you've got to promise to talk to me afterwards."

Jane slid down into the pool of sun on the kitchen floor. She bent her head over the book so that the light shimmered on her hair. Elena watched with her sharp little eyes.

"Ready!" said Jane. "This is for you, remember. It's an old, old story about a little starling who helped a princess."

Elena blinked in surprise, for she was a little starling too. She tipped her head to one side, ruffled her feathers and listened.

"Once upon a time," read Jane, "a beautiful princess called Branwen was kept prisoner in a castle across the sea.

"Every day she had to work in the kitchen. The cook used to beat her. The servants made fun of her. Everyone in the castle was cruel to Branwen, everyone . . . except a little starling who came to her window.

" 'You're the only friend I have, little bird,' Branwen would sigh. 'If only you could talk. Then you could take a message to the giant, my brother.'

"The starling felt sorry for Branwen.

116

He wanted to help her, so he listened and listened till at last he could speak. Then he flew across the sea to a giant as tall as a mountain.

" 'Come quickly!' he cried to the giant. 'Your sister is in trouble!'

"The giant jumped into the waves and walked through the sea to save Branwen. Soon she was sailing safely home, all because of her friend, the starling who had learnt to talk."

Jane put down her book and looked straight at her friend, Elena. Elena's eyes were shining. Suddenly she stepped forward, opened her beak and whistled at the top of her voice.

"Good girl, Elena!" whispered Jane. "You want to learn to talk, don't you, like the starling in the story. Say hello. Hel . . ."

Elena puffed out her chest and whistled her shrill happy whistle.

"No!" said Jane. "Don't whistle. Say hell-o. Listen."

117

But Elena wasn't listening. She wanted to fly to the warm sun that came dancing in through the kitchen window. She stretched out her stiff wings and jumped.

Jane whistled in surprise as the starling swooped over her head with a flutter of wings.

"DAD!" she shrieked. "Daddy!"

Dad came running across the yard. He flung open the door and his great dark shadow filled the kitchen.

"It's Elena!" yelled Jane. "She's better. She's flying."

Elena took one look at Dad and flew up towards him.

"Elena's better!" cried Jane. "Her wing's not all floppy and awkward like it was yesterday and the day before."

Dad reached out his hands, but Elena dodged away and perched on top of the kitchen cupboard.

"She wants to go," he smiled.

"Oh!" Jane stopped in dismay.

Dad pulled a funny face. "We've got to let her go now she's better," he said. "It's

cruel to keep her locked up in the kitchen."

"But I don't want her to go!" cried Jane. "I want to teach her to talk. Starlings are clever, like parrots. Miss Jones said so."

Dad said nothing. He just slid his arm round Jane. They looked up at Elena who was watching the sun ripple through the sprouting branches of the tree outside their window. She whistled with happiness.

Jane whistled back. Elena stared down with her bright beady eyes. She hopped and fluttered and whistled again.

"I think she's saying thank you," Dad whispered. "Thank you, Jane, for looking after my injured wing for the past two days."

Jane rubbed her head against Dad's shoulder.

"No," she said in a small voice.

"No?" said Dad.

"I know what Elena's saying," sighed Jane. "She's saying she wants to go."

She slipped her hand into Dad's and pulled him away from the door. As his shadow disappeared, the sun came streaming into the kitchen.

Elena shivered with joy. She let the sun swoop down her purple feathers. Then, with one goodbye whistle, she flew straight out of the kitchen door. Over the garden wall she surged, on and on until she was just a black speck in the sky.

"Maybe Elena was an overseas starling," said Dad as the tiny black speck disappeared. "The sort that come from colder countries to spend the winter over here. Now that spring has come, she wants to go home." He gave Jane a squeeze. "What do you think?"

"I don't know," said Jane gruffly. "Elena never said a word to me about it."

Dad laughed. And even Jane smiled as she picked up the book from the floor.

"Read this to me," she said, snuggling up to Dad. "It's all about a starling who learnt to talk. It's Elena's story."

But that night, as she winged her way across the sea to her home in Poland, Elena Starling dreamt of a different tale – the tale of a starling princess kept prisoner in a kitchen, a starling princess who'd taught a kind girl to whistle till a great giant Dad came to set her free.

That was Elena's story.

The Little Goldfish

by Geraldine Kaye

When Bo woke up, he smiled at the bedroom ceiling because it was Saturday and he didn't have to go to school. He had been at school in Hong Kong a long time ago, but then his family bought tickets and flew across miles of blue-green sea and now Bo went to school in England and he didn't like it much. He had been at Oak Road School for a term and a bit but he still couldn't speak much English. He knew "okay" and "thank you" and "sorry" and "can't" and as he helped Father in the take-away at night he knew "very quick food" and "what number you want?" but that was just about all.

"Oh, yes, you're the boy from the take-away on the corner, aren't you?" Miss Smith had said on his first day at school. "This is Bo Lee. Who is going to look after Bo Lee for me?" she asked.

"I will," said Charlie, putting up his hand. "I live next door to the Ho Ho Take-Away." Class Two giggled a bit and Bo giggled too, though he had no idea what was funny. "Ho Ho, Bo," somebody whispered. "Ho Ho, Bo."

"Well, it's got Ho Ho Take-Away written over the door," Charlie went on explaining. "And then it's empty space and then it's my house so I can look after Bo easy."

"Thank you, Charlie," Miss Smith said. And Charlie did look after Bo. At "dinner-time" and "playtime" and "singing in the hall" he pushed Bo the way he had to go, but Bo didn't seem to learn much English from being pushed. England was his home now, but somehow it didn't feel like home to Bo.

So Bo was always pleased when it was Saturday and this Saturday there were strange noises coming from outside. He got up and looked out of the window. Below was the back yard and then a fence and then the empty space, but it wasn't empty now. There were lots of lorries and people shouting and dogs barking. What was going on, Bo wondered.

Father and Mother and Elder Sister worked late at night and were still asleep, so Bo ran downstairs and helped himself to *congee*, rice porridge, and tea. Then he went out to the back yard and stood on a box and looked over the fence. There were tents on the empty space now and a merry-go-round with wooden horses and swings and dodgem cars, and now Bo knew what was going on. It was a fair. He had been to fairs in Hong Kong.

Bo spent most of the morning standing on his box, watching the fair being set up. Charlie was wandering round and watching too.

"You coming to the fair?" said Charlie. Bo shook his head.

"Oh, come on," Charlie said. "I'm your friend, aren't I? I'll look after you."

"Friend?" said Bo, not sure he knew the word. "Can't."

"Why not?" Charlie said. "Ask your father if you can come."

"Can't," said Bo.

"I'll ask him, then," Charlie said, and he ran along the pavement and knocked on the side door of the Ho Ho Take-Away.

"Please," he said. "I'm Bo's friend from Oak Road School. Can Bo come to the fair?"

"Friend?" Father said, and Bo wasn't at all sure Father knew the word either, but suddenly Father smiled. "Okay," he said. "Good for son to have friend, good for son to go to fair." And he put a fifty-pence coin into Bo's hand.

"Why do you call it the Ho Ho Take-Away, Mr Lee?" Charlie asked. "It sounds funny in English."

"Ho Ho mean 'excellent' in English," Father said. "What funny?"

"Well, Ho Ho is laughing in English," Charlie tried to explain.

"Laughing Take-Away not okay?" Father said.

"Not okay," said Charlie.

The two boys ran along the pavement. Loud music was coming from the empty space and there were lots of people. The merry-go-round was going round and round and the wooden horses were going up and down.

"Coming on the merry-go-round?" Charlie said, but Bo looked at the silver coin in his hand and shook his head.

"Can't," he said. For a few minutes he watched as Charlie climbed up and got on a wooden horse and then the merry-go-round started.

"Roll up, roll up, four rings to throw for fifty pence!" a man was shouting very loudly, and then Bo noticed the goldfish.

127

Lots of goldfish in a tank. He put his face close to the glass and stared into the greenish water. Back in Hong Kong, Grandfather kept goldfish in a blue and white jar on his bedroom shelf.

"Come along, lad," said the man with the rings. "Four rings for fifty pence and you might win a goldfish."

"Okay," said Bo, and he gave the man his money and threw the rings just as he had in Hong Kong and he won a goldfish. The man scooped a goldfish out of the tank with a net and popped it into a plastic bag.

"There you are, then," he said.

"Can . . ." Bo began, but stopped and blinked because he couldn't think of the right words.

"Can what? Speak up, lad," said the man, and just then Charlie ran up.

"Can the fish live in the plastic bag?" said Charlie.

"Of course not," said the man. "Fish need plenty of water. Take it home and put it into something big."

"Can't . . ." Bo began.

THE LITTLE GOLDFISH

"Tell you what," said Charlie, and his freckled face was all excited. "You stop right here and I'll be back very quick. Okay?"

"Okay," said Bo. He waited, but Charlie didn't come back. He stared at the goldfish in the plastic bag. It swam round ten times, twenty times, a hundred times, and still Charlie hadn't come back. Perhaps Charlie was tired of looking after him, tired of being his friend, Bo thought, and he walked home.

The Ho Ho Take-Away was quiet. Father and Mother had gone shopping. "Fish need plenty of water", the man had said. Bo went into the kitchen and filled the wok with water and put the goldfish in it. The goldfish swam round and round. You could see it quite liked swimming round the wok. But then Father came home.

"The wok is for cooking, son," Father said crossly. "Take that goldfish out."

"Sorry," said Bo, and he popped the goldfish back in the plastic bag and went upstairs to the bathroom. He filled the basin and put the goldfish in. It swam round and round and you could see it quite liked the basin, but then Elder Sister came in.

"I want to wash," she said. "Take that goldfish out."

"Sorry, sorry," said Bo, and he put the goldfish back in the plastic bag. There was a vase on the shelf and he filled it with water and put the goldfish in, but Mother came in.

"Vase is for these flowers, son," Mother said. "Take that goldfish out."

"Sorry, sorry, sorry," Bo said, and he put the goldfish back in the plastic bag and sat down on the stairs.

"Can't . . ." Bo said in a loud voice. "Fish in bag not okay. Fish need plenty of water. Fish need something big."

Downstairs there was a ring at the side doorbell. Charlie stood on the doorstep with something under his arm. He was very pink and out of breath.

"I ran and ran, but you didn't wait," he said. "I had a goldfish bowl at home but it took ages to find it. It's a goldfish bowl for your goldfish, Bo."

"Thanks," said Bo. He filled the bowl with water and popped the goldfish in. You could tell it liked the bowl very much by the way it swam round and round and round. Bo carried the goldfish bowl up to his bedroom and put it on the shelf. A blue and white jar like Grandfather had was good, he thought, but a glass goldfish bowl was even better.

The goldfish bowl is still there, and the little goldfish still swims round and round, and it's the first thing Bo sees when he wakes up. Bo and Charlie are still good friends but Bo knows much more English and he's got quite used to Oak Road School. He still helps Father behind the counter most nights, but now Ho Ho Excellent Take-Away is written over the door.

Den of the Reptile

by Daniel Motsi

This story is set in Zimbabwe, where the winter months are very hot and dry.

In that winter, everything was dry. In the village stream lived only a few frogs that survived in two shallow pools. The frogs croaked the whole night for Mother Nature to have mercy. The grass was dry and the deciduous trees had lost all their leaves. The animals of the whole region's villages trekked far down the dry stream bed to its mouth, where a big river was slowly flowing to the distant sea. Cattle, goats, donkeys and sheep were no longer watched. There are no crops in the fields during winter.

Many of the beasts were as thin as sticks. Some were so weak that they got stuck in the mud when they went to drink the dirty water in the pools. Starved cows often fell on their way to the dip-tank when the thoughtless children drove them too fast. A large pack of wild dogs killed two weaned calves and a goat, then wandered beyond the *kopjes* and the mountain. The pack left the prey half-eaten and the local dogs later spent weeks gnawing the bones.

Murombo, the reigning bull, walked casually among the wandering herd down the stream. His tail swayed with each step. The daily journey to the river for water was very tiresome in hot weather, but they had become used to it. If cattle were able to dig, that year they would have planted a pipeline of water from the faraway river to their *kraals* to make life easier.

All the bathing places in the river were busy in the afternoon. Women brought their clothes and blankets and children to be washed. Some brought wheelbarrows to carry the things. One girl made the journey across the wide river and back in a big dish in which children are bathed. The little girls who were on the bank cheered, clapping their hands. The sailor brought a water lily from the opposite bank.

The cattle drank and returned home, but those which did not live far from the river grazed on the banks, lay on the hot sand or amused themselves with mock battles. Murombo had a drink. While the rest of his herd set off on the journey home, he went down the river's bank to have a little grazing. He was there alone.

The place had that deadly silence that makes us think of all the different things that harm. The sun was about to set. Murombo heard the bellowing of an ox and looked over to the opposite bank. There were other cattle. He hesitated to call with his own voice of power and dropped his head down to graze. When he decided to begin his long journey home, he stepped into the river to take another drink of the wonderful water that was so

scarce in the region.

There was a sudden swirl of water. Murombo roared like a trapped dragon! His leg was in the jaws of a crocodile! The reptile felt the struggle of its victim and was deaf to the cries. Then, as it opened its jaws to get a stronger grip, the crocodile lost its hold. Mud quickly mixed with the water as it groped hither and thither for the escaped prey.

Murombo galloped away in fright, with foam dripping from his mouth. He trotted when going up the dry stream bed, and then slowed down to a walk. Then he stopped and raised his wounded leg, shivering in fear. He turned his head and looked back, wondering what had happened to him. He tried to walk, but ended up limping very slowly along. Blood trickled down to the big hood and dropped on to the dry grass. His heart that had been beating so fast returned to its normal pulse.

It was now dark. Murombo limped into the woodland where there was no wind. He slept beside an anthill that was dense with grass. The following morning he woke up and grazed about, alone like a lost sheep. In the afternoon he was longing for companionship. He bellowed sadly. The sound was quickly sucked up by the woodland. He listened. No answer. Only the guinea fowls chattered as they walked in their family groups, scratching the ground for food and pecking cicadas and other bugs from the tree bark.

He limped back to the dry stream bed and wandered slowly up it, home-ward bound. There was a patch of lovely green weeds near the game path and the bull spotted an almost hidden well in the middle of it.

From his pale grey eyes the water looked clean. Many cattle were now pass-ing him on their way to the river in single file. Some of the cows were even running – not knowing that they were going to the den of the crocodile!

Suspicion Spreads

Folk tale, retold
by Charles Vyas

When there were only animals upon this earth, the elephant was the king of all, and the hare was his adviser. The hare was very fat; the elephant was very thin.

Once the adviser was asked a question, "Why is our king so thin?" Though the question had arisen in private, the elephant heard it. The adviser himself answered the question, "Maybe because he is a king."

This was also said in private, but was heard by the elephant. He thought and thought for days. Then told the hare, "I am thin, perhaps, because I eat leaves and grass."

"You may be right, my King," said the hare with sympathy, and added, "In that case, there's a way out of it."

"How, my adviser? Tell me, how may I grow fat?" asked the elephant anxiously.

"I don't know myself, but we can seek advice from your subjects."

"Yes, yes. Let it be so. Do not delay. Call the animals to a meeting and try to discover the cause as well as the cure."

"That will be done, my King," said the hare, and hurried away.

He sent a message to all the animals. The messenger announced to each of the animals he met, "There is going to be a general meeting tomorrow morning at the king's palace. Each of you must carry with you the kind of food you eat. This will help the king to decide the answer to his problem."

This was heard by all, including a lizard, who decided to pass on the message in his own way. He went off secretly to do this.

On the way, the lizard saw a lion to whom he said, "Oh Mighty Animal, the king has asked me to tell you that it is not necessary for you to attend the meeting. Instead you should guard the kingdom. What he wants from you is a piece of your skin for some magic performance, and that's why I am before you."

The lion obeyed. He scratched off some of his skin and gave it to the lizard to take to the king.

Next, the lizard met a leopard to whom he said, "You, humble servant of the king, you need not attend the meeting, but guard the gate. What the king wants from you is some of your spots for a special use, and that's why I am here before you."

The leopard obeyed. He took off some of his spots, gave them to the lizard to take to the king, and lay bleeding for some time.

Then the lizard stopped an eagle flying and gave an order, "You, the highest flier in the sky, need not attend the meeting. Simply keep a look-out for enemies and go on flying. What the king wants is one of your feathers to use in witchcraft, and that's why I am before you."

The eagle also obeyed. He pulled out a feather and gave it to the lizard to take to the king.

After this, he approached a cat. To this animal he said, "You, the messenger of the king, you need not attend the meeting. You are free to go anywhere you like in the kingdom. What the king wants is some of your whiskers to protect himself from the evil effects of other creatures, and that's why I am before you."

The cat also obeyed.

When the cat disappeared, the lizard shouted at an elephant, "You, kinsman of the king, you need not attend the meeting. After all, you are one of his family. What the king wants from you is your tusk, to give it to a two-legged being to keep him from attacking your people for ever after, and that's why I am before you."

The elephant broke off his tusk and gave it to the lizard to take to the king.

Loading himself up with these articles, the lizard then came to the meeting and sat behind all the other animals present.

The king asked the hare to examine the food the animals were accustomed to eating and to find the type that could make him fat. The hare stood up to carry out the order. While examining the food, he came across the lizard. He asked him to show his food. The lizard showed what he had brought.

"Do you eat these things?" asked the adviser. "If so, it's strange! Very strange! If not, you have insulted the king and you will be dealt with severely for your misconduct."

The lizard requested the hare to hear him patiently. Then loudly he said, "I bow to all of you who have gathered here. You have brought the food you eat. I also had my food with me, but on the way some creatures asked me to carry their food to the meeting, explaining that they were unable to attend the meeting in person. The load was so heavy that I had to drop my food in order to help them in this way."

Saying this, the lizard began to show the articles one by one. First, he showed the lion's skin, holding it up high. Seeing this, the eland got frightened and fled. When he showed the leopard's spots, the monkeys and the antelopes shot off. Seeing the eagle's feather, all the birds disappeared. When he held up the cat's whiskers, the doves and mice made off quickly. Lastly, he showed the tusks to the remaining audience and the king himself left the palace. As he went, the first animal he saw was the lion. To him he said, "I appoint you king of the forest from today, to take over my duties."

Thus the meeting broke up, but fear gripped the animals. Since then they have remained on their guard against their suspected enemies. The eland tries to keep away from the lion, the antelopes and the monkeys from the leopard, the birds from the eagle, the doves and the mice from the cat, and so on.

As for the elephant, because he gave

up the worrying responsibility of kingship, he grew fat. However, he has been trying ever since to keep away from the hunters who make their living by killing his species to get money for the tusks.

Football Revenge

by Julia Eccleshare

Henry hated football. He always had, and he reckoned that he always would. Luckily, no one at home expected him to like it or be good at it or even to play it. But at school all his friends seemed to think it was the best, the greatest, the most important thing in the world.

All playtime long a game of football, or even two or three, would rage up and down the playground. Anyone who didn't want to play got trampled, squashed, pushed or squeezed out of the way. The football tide flowed right up to the benches at one end of the playground and the wire fence at the other end. Even feet got trampled if you left them dangling down from the bench.

Henry was fed up. He had been trying to play transformers with Thomas and Amit and Chia when the football wave crashed over them and scattered everything.

"It's not fair," he told Mum when he got home. "We don't interfere with their football, but they never leave us in peace. And no one ever stops them, because football looks like a proper game."

Mum made lots of suggestions. First she suggested that Henry try playing football. Henry groaned. "I have tried, but I'm no good. No one wants me on their team."

Then Mum suggested playing somewhere else. "We're not allowed anywhere else," said Henry. So she suggested asking the teacher.

"That's no good," said Henry. "Mr Taylor likes football too. He'd never stop it."

Mum finally got tired of making suggestions. "Well," she said. "You'll just have to think up something of your own."

That night, when Henry was in bed, he did some thinking.

His younger brother Edward did some thinking, too.

"You could fight them, bash them all and tie them up in knots," he said, and jumped up and down on the bed to demonstrate the fight, the bash and the knots.

"You could biff all the footballs into outer space." He biffed some odd socks lying on the floor. One landed on top of the cupboard and dangled down just out of reach. The other never even made it into orbit, but dropped on to a Lego model.

"You could cover the playground with Superglue so that they all stick down and can't kick any more." He picked his feet up slowly, showing just how difficult it is to walk or kick in Superglue.

Henry said nothing. He was thinking.

That night, he dreamed of his football revenge.

Instead of a bedside light, Henry had a globe with a light inside. All night long the little globe shone and turned slowly round and round. In Henry's dream, the globe became a football. Not a dirty white plastic football that rolled about and was kicked by anyone who felt like it, but a multi-coloured ball that looked rather like a giant gobstopper. This ball wasn't for anyone to kick. This ball was Henry's, and he alone could control it.

Henry took his multi-coloured football into the playground. He spun it in his hands and then let it stop so that everyone could see that the colours on it came from the different coloured countries on the globe. What nobody except Henry knew was that each colour produced a special effect. Touch red and a red-hot spark shot right through your body. Touch blue and it was like feeling ice – and blue was the most likely colour you could touch, as so much of the world is made up of sea. Yellow gave a jelly-like sensation. First toes, then legs, arms and finally your whole body began to feel soft, wobbly and so helpless that you would collapse in a heap. Green had the opposite effect. Anyone who touched green became still all over and creaky like a rusty robot.

Everyone gathered round Henry.

"Give us a turn."

"Put it down. Put it down. Let *us* have a kick."

"Spoilsport! It's no use to you. You can't even play."

Hands reached out to knock the ball to the ground, but Henry fended them off. He wanted to make quite sure that his revenge would work. He did want everyone to have a kick, but only when he was quite ready.

"Teams," he said quietly. "Make two teams."

There was some shouting and shuffling, and then two teams were grouped together.

"You can be ref," they said.

Henry smiled. He threw the ball high

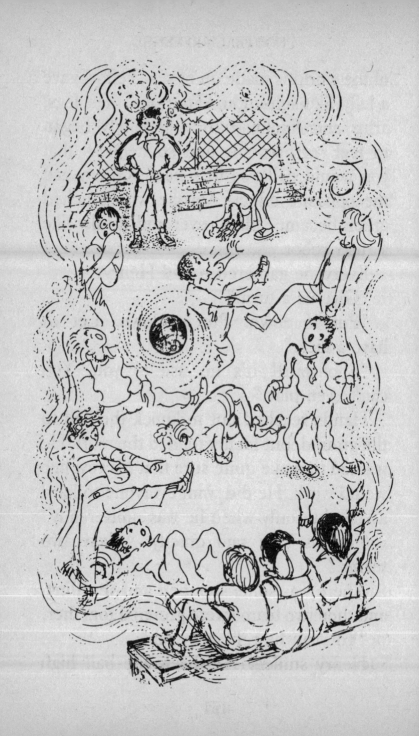

into the air.

"Game begins," he shouted.

Everyone rushed for the ball. Elvin's toe was the first to connect.

"Ow, ow, ow!" he shrieked. "The ball's burning hot!" He retired to the bench.

James had fallen into a heap in the middle of the playground.

"I can't stand," he wailed. He had touched the yellow.

Sean was wobbling in a ridiculous position. One leg was stuck out as it had been when he had first kicked. He was trying hard to get it back to its proper place on the ground, but before he managed it the other players flowed over him and he was knocked over.

Soon there were no footballers left. They had all retired from the game in a huff. Some were rubbing toes or heads which felt as if they had been stung by a wasp or pricked by a pin. Some were trying to get some feeling back into frozen fingers and toes by wriggling them and rubbing them. Some felt stiff and some felt floppy. All of them were cross and confused.

Henry trotted out and collected the ball.

"Dud ball!" Tim shouted at him. "There's something wrong with it."

"No one wants to play football with a rotten ball like that. It bites!" said Alex.

"How come you can hold it OK?" Darren asked.

Henry said nothing. He took the ball and put it in his locker.

The middle of the playground was empty. There was no more football. Henry, Amit, Chia and Thomas played transformers. They could go wherever they liked. Lots of games which hadn't been played for ages started up in the big space in the middle of the playground.

Henry slept well. He slept so well that he overslept in the morning. Mum came in to wake him up.

"Come on," she said. "You can't hide there all day just because of the football."

"I don't mind about football any more. Not at night, anyway," Henry said.

And somehow, from that day on, Henry found that he didn't mind about football in the day so much either, because however bad it was he could always take his revenge at night.

Jets is a series of lively, funny, contemporary stories from some of our most imaginative authors and artists. On every page, illustrations are integrated into the text, making these paperback books ideal for children who are just beginning to enjoy reading.

Houdini Dog by Rose Impey
£2.50
We finally persuaded our parents to let us get a dog – but then we had to choose a name for her. Would we ever agree?

Cowardy Cowardy Cutlass
by Robin Kingsland
£2.50
When Peter gets his hands on a treasure map, it's his big chance to prove himself. All he has to do is get hold of a ship, sail to the island and dig up the loot. But the only ship which will take him is a pirate ship – which wouldn't matter, except they're the weediest, most pathetic pirates ever to sail the seven seas...

Jigger's Day Off by Michael Morpurgo
£2.50
It's harvest time on Mudpuddle Farm, when Jigger the sheepdog has his one day off a year. Just one day to chase all those little animals hiding in the corn. But even the best plans can go wrong.

Josie Smith by Magdalen Nabb

Josie Smith lives with her mum in an industrial town; she is a resourceful, independent little girl who always does what she thinks best, but often lands herself in trouble.

Josie Smith at the Seaside
by Magdalen Nabb

Josie Smith makes friends with a girl called Rosie Margaret; with the donkey, Susie; and with a big friendly dog called Jimmie, who swims off with Josie Smith's new bucket.

Josie Smith at School by Magdalen Nabb

More muddles and misunderstandings for Josie Smith. She is horribly late for lessons when she tries to get a present for her new teacher. And then she helps her new friend to write a story and completely forgets to do her own homework!

Josie Smith and Eileen by Magdalen Nabb

Josie Smith doesn't always like Eileen because Eileen has things that Josie Smith longs for – a birthday party, a bride doll, and the chance to be a bridesmaid in a long shiny pink frock. But Josie is happy in the end.

You can see Josie Smith in the Granada TV serial, *Josie Smith*.

All at £2.75

The Demon Bike Rider by Robert Leeson
£2.25
There was a ghost on Barker's Bonk: a horned demon that made a terrible howling noise as it glided along in the dusk – on a bicycle. Mike and friends thought the bike-riding ghost could only be a joke until they saw and heard it; then suddenly they were running so fast there was no time to laugh.

Challenge in the Dark by Robert Leeson
£2.50
His first week at the new school is a challenge for Mike Baxter – not least when he makes an enemy of Steven Taylor and his bullying older brother, Spotty Sam. But the dare that both accept, of staying in the cold, dark silence of a disused underground shelter, leads to an unexpected friendship.

Wheel of Danger by Robert Leeson
£2.25
When Mike and his friends discover a disused mill out on the moors, it offers an exciting challenge: to get the water wheel working again. But the summer holiday adventure turns to danger when the mill race floods – and three of the children are trapped in the wheel house, with the water rising fast...

Order Form

To order direct from the publishers, just make a list of the titles you want and fill in the form below:

Name ....

Address ....

....

....

Send to: Dept 6, HarperCollins Publishers Ltd, Westerhill Road, Bishopbriggs, Glasgow G64 2QT.

Please enclose a cheque or postal order to the value of the cover price, plus:

UK & BFPO: Add £1.00 for the first book, and 25p per copy for each addition book ordered.

Overseas and Eire: Add £2.95 service charge. Books will be sent by surface mail but quotes for airmail despatch will be given on request.

A 24-hour telephone ordering service is avail-able to Visa and Access card holders: 041-772 2281